CREATION 1954

JOHN GACHICH

This is a work of fiction. All of the characters, organizations, and events portrayed in this novel are either products of the author's imagination or are used fictitiously.

Creation 1954

ISBN: 9798522451660 (trade paperback)

First trade paperback edition: June 2021

*Dedicated to all the men and women who paid
the ultimate price in defense of this nation*

My Beginning

The place was Belgrade, Serbia. The year was 1954, more or less. I was seven years old, more or less. My mother was in the process of teaching me about God and the power of prayer. As a good and obedient son, I listened and followed all her instructions and teachings. I prayed for the health of everyone in my family, including my grand-mother and my dog, both of whom lived in a village about thirty miles from us. I prayed for our neighbors, especially the old guy who lived on the floor below us. This went on for a couple of years, but I really never saw any difference in our lives. The old man died, and I somehow felt a bit responsible thinking that my prayers weren't good enough and I let him down. I always avoided his widow after that for the fear that she may blame me.

That was when I started to question this "God" being and why He didn't keep the old man alive and make my grandmother healthy again. After all, I did what I was told, and He didn't keep His end of the bargain. A few years later, we moved to America and three years after that, my grand-mother died back in Serbia. This time I was truly pissed. Ten years of praying and this is how He treats me? I quit praying and started asking for a sit-down, one on one. I wanted to talk to Him and ask what the problem was. As usual, there was no reply. Time went on and I, more or less, put the sit-down request on the back burner. But I would, from time to time, let

Him know that the issue was still open and that He should at least have the decency to answer me. A few more years passed, and I was drafted into the Army. Following seventeen months of stateside duty, I thought I might get lucky and avoid a Vietnam vacation. Every week or so, the list of those going to Vietnam was posted outside the company clerk's office, and we'd all religiously gather around to see who was going. Not seeing my name on the list, that cool January morning in 1968, I smiled and turned to walk away, when a buddy of mine suggested I look again. As I did, my smile disappeared quickly. I saw the first name on the list. Mine.

During the following fourteen months and three days in Vietnam, I called upon Him several times to see if it would be possible for Him to exert some influence and continue to prevent my demise. I told him that my mother would be very grateful, hoping to elicit some sympathy. While I got no direct answer, and after many hours of combat flight time, I did come home without a scratch none that you could see anyway instilling in me the idea that somehow, I managed to get through to Him and, despite Him not answering, He did hear me. I never did stop asking for a meeting, though, especially after He let me marry and divorce three crazy women. Subsequently, but rather late, I found out about free will, and I quit blaming Him for all the crazy women in my life. By the same token, He could have sent a message of some kind. He's got all those angels at His disposal. Maybe a tap on the shoulder, or as my Kentucky buddies would say, a quick slap upside the head. Nope, no help.

But, looking on the bright side, as a result of my afore mentioned misfortunes, two wonderful kids were added to the population.

Over the years I heard many preachers, priests, and televangelists tell, and some are still telling their parishioners, that God has a plan for them. "Give your life over to God and you will be blessed, and you will be free from worry." That started me thinking. If He has a plan, which, according to these "men of God" was a benevolent plan, why are so many people suffering? Why would He have such awful plans for so many people? Hunger, poverty, disease, war, drought, fires, floods. Why? Did not make sense.

August 20, 2020

I'd first noticed the unusual draft last night, right after I'd settled into my hotel room in Oklahoma City. It had been hot last night, and I figured it was the cheap hotel air conditioning and thought nothing more of it. But the strange draft had persisted throughout the night and into this morning, even as I was driving to the day's project site. It remained there throughout my site visit, and it continued during my ride back to the airport and on my flight back to Chicago. By the time I got off the airplane and picked up my car from the garage, the draft seemed to have disappeared. I wasn't quite sure what to make of the draft. Maybe I was overworked, maybe it was the two flights and six hours in the air that had some effect on me. I tried to put it out of my mind and went to find my car. As I started to pull out of the airport garage like I had so many times before, it returned. This time it was not an air disturbance, but more like a spiritual wind. The draft moved through my head, slowly, left to right. For an instant I thought I was going to faint. It was not painful, not loud, not alarming, and not shocking. It was, in fact, soothing and comforting. And it was clear.

So, you want to talk. I hear you want answers.

This was not some alcohol-induced event. I hadn't had anything to drink that afternoon. Then another message sifted through my mind. Not a voice, but a message.

What answers are you looking for?

People have always told me I'm a little crazy, but this was way beyond the pale. Was I going nuts? Was I hearing things? Had Agent Orange finally cooked my brain to the point that I was starting to hallucinate without herbal or medicinal assistance? And then it came again. No more draft, just the message.

You've been asking questions for over sixty-five years. You said wanted to talk, so talk.

No, this can't be, I thought to myself. Could it really be Him? In a stammer, I managed to form a question of sorts and blurted it out.

"You know it's night and I'm driving, right?"

I have no idea where you are or what time it is. I just know you have questions. So ask.

"Okay, listen, I don't know what kind of game this is, but I am tired and need to get home in one piece and get some rest."

If I tried to talk to God right then and there, I'd most likely wreck the car.

I can't wait for you humans to start using some more of those thinking brain cells I gave you. Maybe then I'll be able to have a somewhat intelligent conversation with one of you. The last guy I tried to help was babbling something about a burning bush and stone tablets. I gave him the tablets as he requested. I even wrote down what he asked. Apparently, he thought that the message would carry more weight if the people were told the message was from me. After all I did for him, he had the gall to throw the tablets at his brother, just because the brother fashioned some cockamamy golden calf, threw a big shindig, and got people drunk. As penance I made him carve new tablets and present them to his people. He wasn't pleased.

"The Ten commandments, right?"

Of course, it's the Ten Commandments, you putz. Boy, you people are irritating. You know, I don't have time for this nonsense now. Go home, get some rest, and I'll be in touch in the morning.

Then the breeze and the messages were gone. I drove home thinking that I was overworked, tired, and had imagined the whole thing.

August 21, 2020

Morning came, I went next door for breakfast without really thinking about what transpired the night before. I came back home and tried to relax with my second cup of coffee when the draft returned, accompanied by a new message.

Okay, let's try this again. Are you awake?

"Yes, yes, I am."

Are you ready to talk? I don't do this often, so use your time wisely, and if you are planning to tell someone about this, make sure you take good notes. Otherwise, they may think your axis is skewed a few too many degrees to the left. In other words, they will think you are nuts.

Straining to believe who I was talking to, I suddenly realized that I was not actually hearing Him speak nor was I actually speaking in return. It was all taking place in my mind. I grabbed my notebook and managed to mumble a reply.

"No, no, I'm keeping good notes."

> *Continuing on about that Moses guy and his tablets. I just called them the Ten Laws, but he insisted on the Ten Commandments. He thought the people would obey them more willingly if we changed the name, and he asked if it was okay for him to tell his people that these Commandments came from me. Against my better judgement, I agreed and the rest, as they say, is history.*

"Wait, wait, wait. You remember things you did four thousand years ago, and you are supposed to be all seeing and all knowing, but you didn't know I was driving last night. You didn't even know it was night. How am I supposed to take this seriously? What in holy hell is this?"

> *Whoa! Easy chum. Be respectful. Do you know who I am?*

"Sorry, forgive me, but at this point I can only make a guess."

Ah, right. Let's get that part out of the way. First things first. I am the Creator of what you call the Universe but, contrary to what you might have heard, I am not all knowing and all seeing, and while I am the Creator of the said Universe, I cannot see everything and be everywhere at all times. Let me give you some reference so you can see exactly where you fit into the whole thing. The first thing you need to understand is that there are seven sectors in this Universe and each sector has four quadrants totaling twenty eight. Assisting me in the original creation and subsequent administration of these seven sectors, I have seven assistants who help me in keeping things moving forward. For reference, since many of your early texts call them angels, I'll refer to them as such. I just call them my A's, A1 through A7, and I picked them from a myriad of candidates. After all, creating the Universe could not be trusted to just anyone. It took a long time to create all this and keeping track of all of it is an immense undertaking. As big as the Universe is, I cannot be in all places at all times, so I rely on my seven chosen angels.

Second, I get reports from the A's about progress in the various sectors, and the eight of us get together from time to time so they can bring me up to date on what is happening in various locations. From

*time to time means every few thousand years.
Since evolution is very slow, there is not much
progress to report on a shorter time period. You
understand?*

"I think so. A lot of us were told that the world was created
in six days. So, what you are saying is that's wrong?"

*Really? You have all this science behind you, and
you ask that question? You know about the big
bang, you know about the dinosaurs, you know
how the continents move around, you know that
Earth's inner central core is solid iron, and the
outer core is molten iron and rock, you know that
the Earth moves around the Sun, yet you ask if
it was all created in six days? You know that the
Universe is expanding, you know about black
holes actually you don't know much about black
holes, but that's a topic for another time. You can
measure the speed of light, yet you ask if it was all
created in six days! Hell no, it wasn't created in
six days! At least not days like you think of them.
In your religious texts, the word "day" is given a
meaning far beyond what mortals perceive a day
to be. A day is described to mean a long period of
time some call it an eon in those texts. This can
then explain more accurately the length of time
it took to create "the heavens and the earth." Of
course, accurate is a relative term here since you*

people still insist on creating weapons of war instead of trying to better yourselves. Your scientists have calculated the Universe to be approximately 13.8 billion years old, which is close to correct, but I cannot say for certain since I lost my notes in that big explosion. Six days is a metaphor because when those texts were written, few people could read and most had to take off their sandals to count past ten. Trying to get anyone in those days to comprehend a number of that magnitude would have been impossible.

But I digress. Anytime someone mentions a "day" it sets me off. Getting back to your original questions, why did you want to talk to me?

"Oh right. I wanted to know why my prayers weren't working. Why did my grandmother not get better? Why did my old neighbor die even though I prayed for him all that time? But then I got older, and I realized that it wasn't that my prayers weren't getting answered but the fact that all living things die. So, we don't have to worry about that question right now. What I want to know is why you didn't at least answer the request for a sit-down? I asked so many times that I thought I would lose some of my brain cells."

I'm glad you figured out the first one by yourself. Congratulations. By the way, most people figure that one out by the age of eight or nine, so don't think you're too smart. Now the sit-down question is a little puzzling to me. You are some kind of builder or architect, which means you have to be very proficient in math. Yet the fact that, with minimal assistance, I am in charge of the whole Universe, seems to elude you. In the past 14 billion years or so I've had to get all the preparations done for the Second Burst, get as many pieces of the puzzle as possible, ready, and in place, so that life would flow forth, and finally, initiate the explosion. This wasn't some kid's bar mitzvah we were planning. I wasn't worried about some caterer not bringing that special pickled herring Uncle Moishe likes so much. This was a big deal. Again, a big deal.

"I understand it was a big deal. No reason to be condescending, I understand the difference between colossal and trivial."

Fine, you are smart.

"Again?"

Quit interrupting. Actually, it was the second big deal of my career. The first one was not as successful as advertised. When it blew up, it wasn't a nice spherical blast. It went to one side and turned into a fat banana-shaped affair, with dust and rocks flying every which way. We couldn't get gravity to take hold and start pulling pieces together, there wasn't a lot of light, and it was much colder than we expected. Yeah, the seven assistants were there. They were all eagerly anticipating getting their own sectors to look after but wound up staring at this banana-looking thing and trying to figure out who was getting what and how that thing was going to get divided. After a couple of million years and before the whole thing got any worse, I decided to pull the plug, recall the whole thing, and go back to the drawing board. That's a human phrase, by the way.

"Thanks for telling me, I never heard that before."

Sarcasm duly noted. Now be quiet.

You think your notion of herding cats is difficult, try putting a nonconforming Universe Great Burst, back into the bottle. We had to do it all ourselves, no neighbors out there. It was a nightmare, but after four plus million years we managed to bring most of the pieces back together for a second try. Hence the name, Second Burst. You guys call it the Big Bang because you just don't know the whole history. In case you didn't get the gist of what I explained above, if you try to calculate the amount of work that I was saddled with, there wasn't time to contact one millionth of one percent of the people trying to get something from me. You also should not worry about losing brain cells through multiple attempts trying to make contact. We gave you plenty of spares, knowing that many of you would partake heartily of herbs and drink that nature made available. If spares were not provided, many of your kind would have become blithering idiots very quickly, and I cannot be reversing this Burst at this stage in order to fix your shortcomings.

"I get it. You're busy. And from what you just said, you and the A's obviously possess powers and abilities beyond human comprehension, which leaves me wondering. Why would you go out of your way to help some shepherd with the carving of some tablets?"

Yeah, well, we all make mistakes. But given the situation back then, it seemed like a good idea. We didn't have much experience with somewhat primitive people at that time and were of the opinion that we could help. The resulting consequences taught us not to interfere ever again.

I started to notice that every time I mentioned anything related to Moses, He got a little touchy, but I was still curious about the Ten Commandments.

"I would like to follow up on those tablets, is that okay?"

Sure.

"You said that you helped Moses with tablets, and he wasn't grateful. I'm assuming you know how that story was written."

Of course, I know how it was written, and although I said I was not all knowing and all seeing, I know a lot and I have seen a lot. And when I say a lot, I mean a lot. And I told you about my assistants who can fill me in on things I may have forgotten. When you get to be almost 15 billion years old, you tend to not remember as well as when you were 12 billion. Go on.

"How much of that story is true?"

Well, you know how publicity skews everything. Happens now. Happened then. I carved the tablets for him, and he got real pissed at his brother Aaron and threw the tablets at him, which in turn upset me, and I made Moses carve a new set. I realized later that he was an old man and was prone to getting upset easily, something akin to your neighbor Benny who keeps telling kids to get off his lawn. I think he was over eighty at that time, and eighty was very old then. He had just led the Hebrews out of bondage and endured all that stuff with the Pharaoh, and all that travel leaving

Egypt. Having been a Prince of Egypt and being somewhat arrogant, he embellished that thing about the parting of the Red Sea. The portion of the Red Sea they crossed was just a slip of water at that time, with an ancient bridge connecting the two shores. Moses told the people to get across the bridge quickly because the Pharaoh's chariots were gaining on them rapidly. And when the people were safely on the other side, Moses had Aaron, Joshua, and a couple of the bigger well-fed boys jump into the water and loosen the bridge supports. Sure enough when the Pharaoh's chariots reached that part of the bridge, the supports gave way and they all wound up in the water. Moses then told the people he had summoned God to part the waters and destroy the chariots. That was one of the first political stump speeches in history. Moses thanked them for their support and informed them that he was going to meet God on some mountain to receive God's law. Just as the A's and I were getting ready for a rare moment of relaxation, he came up, interrupted our picnic, and asked for the tablets. To get rid of him, and so we could continue with our picnic, we gave him what he wanted. Apparently, he had some dream of being a big wheel in the Hebrew community, so he employed some tactics that weren't up to the standards of the Commandments he requested. One of those was the fable that he fathered a son when he was ninety-two, trying to emulate Abraham who allegedly fathered a son when he was one hundred years old. That's when the terms "not Kosher" and "limp noodle don't dance" were coined. Does that clear it up?

"For the most part. Thank you. I would like to go in a different direction if that's okay."

If you must.

"This may be a little naïve on my part, but how does one become the Creator? I'm guessing you didn't answer an ad in the Cosmic Times that some organization was looking for a Director of Universe Creation."

Ladies and Gentlemen, we have a comedian among you. Thank you for that question, and I am glad that you feel comfortable asking it in a such a humorous way. Ha, ha. Obviously, there was no ad, you putz. At the instant of my existence, that would be like birth to you, I was presented with the task of Creation. Maybe not presented. I just knew. The same way a hen knows to sit on fertilized eggs, although my task was a bit more complex.

"What? You didn't get an instruction manual?"

Another joke! That's two in a row. No, there were no instructions. I didn't have any plans. You are an architect, you know you can't build without plans. Not something that will last. I had so many questions. However, I felt that this was my purpose and for some reason I had no hesitation, no trepidation, and no apprehension. Just a feeling of a mission that had to get done. Failure was not an option. Yes, Hollywood stole that one from me. Since I was all alone, I knew I would have to figure out the how, where, and when. Why, as a concept, did not present itself until my existence was well into double digit billions of years. More on that later. Realizing that this effort would be difficult to achieve alone, the first thing I did was supply myself with assistants. I created a whole bunch of them because I knew that the task ahead would be immense. I'm not sure how I did it though. It was instinctual, just like your birds knowing they need to fly south in the winter, but it was amazing.

I didn't concern myself with the small details. The mission of Creation was paramount. Out of many I picked only the seven best. Seven extremely capable entities of immense and diverse capabilities. Once we had our team in place, I had to devise methods of communication across incalculable distances, methods of energy and matter creation, collection, gathering and finally, release.

This task was and is never-ending, thankless and exhausting and, as you are witness, it continues to this day. It could be compared to back when you were with your third wife, and you thought having your mother-in-law living with you was a chore. Just think of living with her for 15 billion years. Now that would be a chore. How would that feel, Mr. Architect?

I wasn't about to utter a word. Ten years was bad enough, so I certainly wasn't about to open another can of worms. Besides the only more welcome sight than your mother-in-law leaving is seeing her daughter follow right behind her. Yet somehow, I felt that God was really not looking for an answer here, and the whole concept of angel and energy creation intrigued me enough that I had to ask.

"Where did all that energy come from? I mean gathering all the matter and energy needed to create the Universe and get it to a single location is a major undertaking."

Sure, start with simple questions first. Okay, listen carefully. The energy came from me. Remember I was and continue to be the Creator, and I do have capabilities. We developed a cosmic transport system that allowed movement of massive amounts of matter by imbuing energy into that matter, subsequently directing that energy-imbued matter to a specific location. Similar to how auto factories move cars along an assembly line run by computers, on your world. My task was on a slightly larger scale. Now it's time for you to put on your calculator hat and imagine the magnitude of what I just said. Again, listen carefully. I am talking about transporting enough matter, which when properly processed, compressed and combined with the requisite proportional amount of energy, would wind up comprising hundreds of thousands of galaxies. No, no, wait, billions and billions of galaxies. To summarize, we had to put together a system of matter collection, perform that previously mentioned energy imbuing, and transport it all to the detonation point, in other words, where we were going to blow it all up. Luckily, we didn't have any regulations or environmental concerns since we hadn't yet created the environment. Actually, that would be, environments, since there would eventually be so many different ones, and if we did our job correctly, we would create some that would produce life. Just think about trying to do that today. I'm getting ahead of myself here and again I digress, do forgive me. You with me so far?

"Yes, yes. Please go on."

This galactic transport lasted well over six million years. Finding storage at the "burst" location was an absolute nightmare. As soon as the disgruntled angels that's how I refer to the ones I did not select found out where the storage facility was, they started leaving their spare wings all in our way.

"Angels actually have wings?"

Of course. They have to be able to move about, but their mode of travel is not as advanced as ours. So yes, some of your early scribes actually got that one right.

Moving on. We finally worked out a deal where they would store their wings far away from the planned burst location and we would provide some no-show flying jobs for some of their friends after our task was completed. By the way, that was when the first unions were formed. They said we were being exploitative and engaged in unfair labor practices.

"All of this is really difficult to absorb and while I consider myself fairly intelligent, but this is very mind boggling, as it does not coincide with how our existence was explained to us. You see, in physics classes we were taught that there was nothing before the Big Bang. Sorry, Second Burst. How is it possible for nothing to exist before and now all of this exists afterwards?"

Actually, it did exist. We just had the benefit of knowing where to look. Like the birds. On Earth and other planets, there are birds that will travel hundreds of miles in search of food for their young, knowing that they will be successful. Just like those birds, we knew we would find the matter. Once it was located, we brought it all to the "burst" location and proceeded with our mission. Now just because some astrophysicist tells you his theory that all the matter in the Universe "could have arisen from a bit of primordial energy weighing no more than a pea," you are going to believe him? I, with my seven angels, spent over six million years collecting, compacting, infusing all that energy into the galactic matter, transporting it all to the "burst" location, and some balding guy in a cheap suit who finally figured out how tuning forks work is going to tell me that all of that weighed as little as a pea? Over six million years and we moved a pea. I also heard that this same guy theorized that before the Second Burst, the Universe was filled with unstable energy which, by some fashion, was "transformed into the fundamental particles" in an instant, and all matter in the Universe arose from that event. This is what your geniuses call the Big Bang. Unstable energy, my ass. All the energy in the Universe was located inside all the matter and it was not unstable. It was very stable, and we made sure that after the First Burst, everything was properly located so when the second expansion took place it would be somewhat even and would not produce the Banana Universe disaster, we created the first go round. Looking at the age and shape of this Burst, we accomplished what we set out to do, albeit on the second attempt. And for your information, all energy stored in the matter at the time of the Second Burst is still contained within it and cannot leave. That way, if need be, we can activate the energy stored within the galactic matter and direct individual planets, stars, comets or other celestial bodies to go where they need to go. Does that clear up everything for you? Are you ready for more?

I was definitely ready for more. I'd been waiting for this conversation my entire life.

"Definitely. Let's go back to history. In the holy books of the major religions, most, if not all events are played out in what is currently the Middle East. Why is that?"

Ah, the Middle East. Well, there's no real reason. We just happened to be there at that time I guess it was about four or five thousand years ago as we were doing one of our rounds of the Universe.

We make these rounds of the living planets every five to six thousand years to see how sentient life is progressing. The planets that are just starting, we visit once every three to four hundred thousand years. No need for any more frequent stops since we know nothing significant happens in the first couple of billion years anyway. When we do visit, we usually stay about fifty to a hundred years to see what our "people" have wrought. We happened to "land" in that area at the time and took an interest in those folks. I remember there was lots of hate going on at the time, people enslaved, lots of killing, robbing, you name it. We usually don't interfere in planetary matters because it could skew the evolutionary process, but these people were going nuts, so we decided to stick around a while longer to see if the situation warranted our attention.

"So, you helped the Jews because you felt sorry for them?"

They weren't called Jews back then, but yes. There were many families, tribes, tongues, lineages, religions and beliefs that needed to be sorted out, and we felt we had no choice but to get involved. In retrospect, we should have just left and let evolution do what it does best. Separate the wheat from the chaff and let nature rule. But we thought we were the smart ones. Hey, we created the Universe, we can straighten out a few errant sheep herders. Unfortunately, those people were crazy. We gave them a little more brain power than they were capable of utilizing and they blew it. One side said we are descendants of Abraham through Isaac, the other guys said we are descendants of Abraham through Ishmael, and because one guy was older, we are the "older sons." This "issue" still persists today even though they are both descended from the same grandfather. Same Goddamn Blood. Same. Same. Same. How many times does it need to be said? If you want to know more about our screw up, read the Bible and the Quran. You'll get to see many branches and many leaves of the same tree, yet somehow the people have not yet been able to come to grips that if you have the same ancestor, you are related, you are one. Kapish?

"Kind of. No, not really. If we're all related, why are there so many different races? How did that happen?"

Here I am spending precious time with you and the more I talk the dumber you get. How does that happen? You really should read the Bible and the Quran and gain some insight on that issue. Those two books are a good starting place where you can learn some of the basics, in that, man was created in the image of God. That, however, is not how all of those who wrote the texts interpreted that part of Creation. It also does not mean that you humans look like God. That means God's image of what you should be like, not necessarily what you should look like.

"Hold on, let me digest this. You are telling me that the reason we look the way we look was nature's doing?

Yes. You catch on quickly. All we did was create the circumstances for life to evolve. What it looked like at the end of the journey was not up to us, it was up to nature. We supplied the soil, water and sustenance which allowed the tree to grow. What that tree looked like in the end was not our concern, only that it was viable, capable of reproducing, and well suited for its environment. That means location. That is why there are many different trees, and races, and all are glorious. Not just on Earth but across the Universe. If you look around, not all trees are green, some are yellow and some are red and some are purple, and none is less magnificent than another. If only I could get the humans to understand that, you would be well on our way to, what Buddha calls, enlightenment.

"Wait, wait. Just so I'm clear, by "we" you mean the seven A's and you, with you being the main force being it all."

Correct. It was not easy creating the Universe, seeding it with life, weeding it of our mistakes, correcting trajectories of billions and billions of fast moving celestial objects, and maintaining it all, without help. Things get really tense when certain of those celestials defy the laws of physics and decide to go rotate in a non-prescribed manner. Sometimes I just want to blow something up again but that can present unintended consequences and is obviously counterproductive. We have to co-exist. We also have to keep traffic flowing by making sure that galaxies don't collide in another catastrophic event. Yes, it has happened before, and it wasn't pretty. Now when we see that galaxies are on a collision course, we provide what you would consider gravitational brakes and allow them to mesh rather than collide whereby two smaller galaxies become one big one. That's where the black holes come in. They swallow up as many errant stars, planets, comets and other space debris that could possibly interfere with cosmic traffic and provide for a smooth gradual interlacing of celestial elements. We constantly have envoys on the lookout for extra-terrestrial objects that could do damage to the important parts of the Creation such as your planet, also the more advanced ones, and the ones that show real promise.

"Wait, there are other planets that are more advanced than us?"

And to think I took time out from hanging out with A3 and A6 to come and talk to you. You know, putz is too nice of a nickname for you. I'll think of something more appropriate and let you know.

"I'm sure you will."

Don't be impertinent. Of course, there are other planets that are more advanced than Earth. You think that I could get another Creator position if all I had to show on my resume was this excuse for a planet. Look at your sorry lot. We gave you a nice blue planet and you are filling my oceans with plastic and garbage. You keep fighting wars after we warned you last time we were here that wars only lead to more wars. A few years ago, you discovered the power of the atom and you thought you were it. Bullshit! Now everybody and their brother has an atom bomb, and worse, you feel it necessary to build even more destructive weaponry. Recently, it was brought to my attention that two or three of your tribes or countries, whatever you call them, have the ability to destroy the planet three times over. For this, you were given a brain? For this, the seven Angels and I created nature and within it, evolution, which in turn got you to walk upright, have the intelligence to figure out how to clothe yourself, house yourself, have five senses and provided you with a wife, or in your case, three wives, so you would not have to procreate by yourself, although some of you apparently prefer that. For all that was given to you, this is what we get in return? Should have told evolution to leave you walking on all fours. Nature would do what she does, and the animals would be happy with no one present to build shopping malls, highways and amusement parks to encroach into their habitat.

I understood that God was upset, but I wasn't to blame.

"I'm just one old man. Why are you taking it out on me?"

Because you piss me off and there is no one else around to hear me. I know, you don't like to hear all this and that's too bad. You kept pestering me for over sixty-five years about a sit down, you wanted answers, you wanted reasons, and you wanted explanations. Now that you are getting them, you get upset that I'm taking it out on you. Next time don't be such a pest and maybe you'll fare better.

I waited, unsure what to say that wouldn't send Him into another hissy fit.

I do apologize for that tirade, I don't know what got over me. Actually, I do. I look at this magnificent gift of a planet, and you people don't take care of it.

"I know. Many people have raised major concerns, but agreements among countries are very difficult to come by. Mainly due to everybody trying to be the big dog and possessing an overblown, egotistical sense of self-worth. It's beyond frustrating. But can we talk about these other planets some more? You said there are more advanced planets. Exactly how much more advanced are they?"

Some of these things you are not going to comprehend, so let me point you in a scientific direction where you can educate yourself and not depend on me coming to force feed you that, which you should already know. On Earth you have and have had a number of extremely brilliant physicists and scientists. Not all that many, but brilliant none the less. Einstein, Franklin, Fowler, Feynman, Fermi, Tesla, Sagan, Tyson

"Mike Tyson?"

No, you moron, Neil deGrasse Tyson. What are you, twelve? Look him up.

You know, because of your age, I thought you would be a little more refined, but apparently, your Balkan side is showing.

"Okay, okay, okay. So now we are down to insults. Wait 'til I start asking questions about some of your masterpieces like mosquitos, kangaroos, mice, and that pecker nosed monkey from Borneo. Anyway, back to the scientists."

Right. Tyson, Bell yes, the telephone guy Kaku and a number of others. I don't have time or the inclination to name all of them. No, not because I don't know all the names but because you are going to start busting my chops and accusing me of being a know-it-all and a show-off. Obviously, you have heard of Einstein, Sagan, Fermi and a few others, I'm sure.

"You don't have to talk down to me. All I want is information, and you are the ultimate source. And of course, I've read about Einstein, Tesla, Kaku and some of the others. I'm not a moron."

It just seems that at your age you should know a lot more about how the Universe works.

"I'm sorry, I am an immigrant. I learned English in high school, I had to go to war, I was married three times, and one of my kids won't talk to me. But I know stuff. I bet I know stuff that you don't even know."

Oh yeah? Tell me something I don't know.

"Well, do you know that Nikola Tesla was Serbian?"

Of course, I know that. Everybody knows that.

"Aha. Now I know you haven't kept up with the times. Yes, everybody should know that, but very few do. Scientists know, but the average guy walking down the street? Not a clue. When you tell them that he is the father of alternating current, they look at you like you are nuts. I've met electricians who don't know. 'Who?' they say. 'He invented what?' They don't believe you. Also, do you know that Einstein was married to a Serbian woman?"

Seriously? That I did not know. Are you pulling my leg?

"No joke. Mileva Marić. Look it up. Ha, ha, ha. They went to school together. She was brilliant, even got better grades than old Albert and helped him write some of his papers. So, I know things. Now let's go back to these scientists. Is there anybody I should look up in particular? Wait, wait, did you say pulling my leg?"

Never mind the leg thing, we'll talk about that at the end if we have time. As for the scientists, one guy that stands out to me is Michio Kaku. Without actually knowing, he explains the possibilities of evolutionary development in the Universe, and what that could look like, in very simple and understandable terms.

"Okay, lay it on me."

Lay it on me? Now there's something I haven't heard since the sixties. Again, listen carefully. Paraphrasing now.

Think of all the advancements we have made in the last 100-150 years. Electricity, indoor plumbing, planes, trains, dams, high-rise buildings, agriculture, medicine, etc. Imagine all the things we didn't have just a century ago and where we are now. Then imagine a society or civilization that is 100 years ahead if us. What kind of planes, ships, computers, and other wizardry would they have? Just imagine.

You ready? Now, imagine if they are one million years ahead of you. What would that look like?

Hard to wrap your brain around, don't you think? By the way, who came up with this "wrap your brain around it" saying?

"I have no idea, but it's a very common phrase today. Probably one of those smart scientists while taking a hiatus from figuring how the Universe works."

Ha! That's a good one. And you may be right. Every now and then they need a break from all that hard thinking. It really puts a strain on the brain. You see what I did there? Strain on the brain?

"It's good to see you do have a sense of humor. And I do see what you did there."

I have to have a sense of humor to deal with you clowns.

And it sure would have been nice if my math angel, A6, added an extra factor into his evolution calculations. You would be at about 40-45% brain thinking capability by now, and this trip would have been much more educational for you and me. Sure, I know that many of your scientists say that the brain is working all the time, but a lot of that is expended on keeping you fed, rested, walking without falling, staying out of the rain, taking a crap, and other everyday needs. The thinking part

.

34

*is where you fall short and are still way behind
some of the other folks in the fourteenth quadrant.*

"Just a quick tidbit from my Vietnam days. I'm not so sure
about that 'staying out of the rain' part. It doesn't activate as
quickly as it is supposed to in some people. One day, while
in Vietnam, I found one of our pilots standing on the flight
line, in the rain, outside of a locked aircraft, thinking that
the crew would be joining him momentarily. He was soaked
to the bone and apparently had forgotten an all-important
fact. That being, we only flew in the rain in extreme emer-
gencies or in case of attack. Later, I heard, he committed a
different and more egregious error, one that could have had
serious, maybe even fatal, repercussions and was promptly
sent elsewhere. This time to the supply company where he
would help distribute boots, uniforms, and underwear to
the troops. Someplace where a screwup would only result
in someone having to wash his drawers by hand instead of
going home in a box. And this guy was an officer and a pilot.
Makes you wonder. Anyway, I digress. Please continue."

*I hope you understand my frustration with you
people now. Your example is well-taken and shows
that you people need a lot of work. I haven't been
here in more than forty centuries and the only
thing that has really progressed is your ability
and capacity to wage war. You know, those other
advanced planets managed to avoid self-destruc-
tion. There are ways to avoid it, but you all have to*

be onboard and committed. Otherwise, I'm pretty sure that if you stay on this path, you will cause extreme harm to the planet and basically remove yourselves from existence, as you know it. Maybe not totally remove, but certainly take yourselves back many centuries. Think back to working the land manually and plowing the fields with beasts of burden, no electricity, no running water, no machines of any import, having to learn everything all over again, without teachers. Re-live all those failures of the past that did not need re-living. That is your future which awaits. Your future is your past.

"That would not be good for us, but maybe the planet would prosper."

When you are right you are right, although not having you people around would make our existence much less entertaining. Watching you elect moron after moron to essential and important positions is better than watching Jerry Springer but, then again, I ask myself, what have we wrought? Maybe on the next planet expecting human-like creatures to evolve, we'll dispense with that step and just keep the "lower" animals. They live by nature's code and will not harm or try to destroy their celestial gift.

You know that before humans set foot on Earth there were five planet wide extinctions that were caused by either geological or cosmic events. Granted, we were involved with the asteroid one which rid the planet of dinosaurs and gave you the chance to develop and evolve, but the other ones were completely by chance.

"Yes, I've read about those. Scientists are still trying to figure some of those out, but it was such a long time ago, I'm not sure how successful they will be."

At least you are trying. That gives me hope.

After what appeared to be a compliment, I was afraid that God might go off on one of his tirades again, so I figured I better get the conversation back on track.

"Let me get back to these advanced planets in the fourteenth quadrant. If they are more advanced than we are, then they must be older than Earth. Did I get that right?"

Yes, you are correct, there are two. Planets Number 14-347 and 14-444, but 14-347 is the one that is really thriving. You are not as much of a putz as I thought, after all.

"Thank you."

Don't interrupt. That's pretty much how it works. The earlier you are born the sooner you mature and the sooner you die, although, that does not necessarily apply to planets. I seem to recall hearing about that concept somewhere, but I forget. It's tough when you are fifteen billion years old, some things just slip away.

"Sure, I'll bet. Incidentally, whatever happened to that breeze you sent my way in the beginning?"

Again, with the mouth. You are lucky I am way past the smiting period of this journey with Creation, otherwise I would show you a thing or two.

And the breeze was needed to get your attention, I needed you to sense something. I didn't want you having a heart attack at the first message.

"Sure, sure, now I see. You keep harping on man's constant obsession with war, but the minute I throw you a zinger that you don't care for, you want to resort to smiting."

I said I was past it, didn't I? Let's move on to the important stuff.

Back to the living planets. There are two in the fourteenth quadrant that are more advanced than you and one that is not. The one that is not,

14-167, is about four thousand years behind you. Essentially, they are developmentally at the same place Earth was about the time of that Moses guy, more or less. They know how to farm, build, write, and wage war, although they are not as enamored with war as Earthenites were back at that stage of their development. Yes, the word Earthenites is a real word, and it is the correct word. That is what A7 called your people and it stuck. I've also heard you called Earthlings, but to me it sounded more like something a goat would leave behind after a heavy meal, so I discouraged its use.

"Wait, what is our planet number?"

14-297.

"Right. And do the other planets in the fourteenth quadrant have names like normal planets?"

Actually, no. Your people decided to call your planet Earth, while the others, being so much more advanced, used our numbering system in keeping with their high technology culture. Besides, we don't just number the planets, we number all celestial bodies in the Universe. Do you have any idea how many names would have to be concocted and recorded in the great celestial books to be tracked? Trillions. That is why we use numbers.

Keeping track of trillions of names is just not practical. For a long time, you had only nine but apparently that must have been so difficult that one of them got demoted.

When I heard that I almost fell on the floor laughing. So to speak. I can't really fall and there is no floor where I am. I heard that some "scientists" redefined what a planet was and promptly removed Pluto from the planet ranks. I spend all that time and expend all that energy creating Pluto, and some more, seemingly educated, putzes come along and say that what I created is not a viable planet. Here is their interpretation of what a planet is. Verbatim. The International Astronomical Union defines a planet as "a celestial body that (a) is in orbit around the Sun, (b) has sufficient mass for its self-gravity to overcome rigid body forces so that it assumes a hydrostatic equilibrium (nearly round) shape, and (c) has cleared the neighborhood around its orbit." If you don't believe me, take a look at the Sky and Telescope website, it's right there.

Okay, let's break this down.

(a) is in orbit around the Sun

That sounds reasonable. It must have been the tough one to figure out, but okay.

(b) has sufficient mass for its self-gravity to overcome rigid body forces so that it assumes a hydrostatic equilibrium (nearly round) shape

Wow. How about, round, spherical or just "nearly round." I guess that would have been too simple. I'll bet not one of those pencil necks could recite that definition without reading it from his little My Guide to the Planets handbook.

(c) has cleared the neighborhood around its orbit

Now they don't like the neighborhood. They want the planet to get rid of its neighbors so when said pencil necks visit, they can tell their mother-in-law the neighborhood is safe. Really? You actually live with these people?

To make matters worse, they classified my Pluto as a dwarf planet. A dwarf planet. The gall of these people. It's a good thing they are not in charge of classifying people. No, no don't tell me, I don't want to know.

I kind of zoned out during His Pluto tirade. My mind was stuck back on something else He'd said.

"Wait, wait. There are celestial books?"

No, dummy, it's a figure of speech.

"Oh."

Don't be sad. I can make you a book.

"Really?"

No not really. Now can we get on with it?

"Sure. I thought you liked scientists?"

*I do, but the ones who tell you how smart they are
and won't show you their college transcripts aren't
my cup of tea. Just like your politicians. I'll bet you
didn't think I knew about those guys. Earth is not
unique in that respect. We have these pests on the
other three planets also. Actually, some of them
are decent beings but unfortunately, you won't
live to see the appearance of that miracle on your
planet. I've seen that trend before on other planets and as I've said previously, you guys are not
unique.*

"Do you really follow our politics?"

Of course. The better the governing bodies and institutions the more prosperous the people. Better science, better health, more imagination and better understanding of the gift you were given. You are well aware what dictators and tyrants are capable of. Now turn that 180° and imagine that scenario. Sunshine all day and rain at night, friendly neighbors and green pastures, forests everywhere you look and birds singing in the morning. Glorious, don't you think?

"Sure, but does a place like that actually exist?"

Nope. Some are better than others, but none is remotely close to perfect. Like with the Moses thing, we tried and found out that meddling in your and others' affairs just doesn't work. Once a group gets your help, they figure you are on their side and against the others. They don't realize that all are part of Creation and all need embracing. But, as usual, everybody wants more than the other guy, and the friction never dissipates. They are all willing to sacrifice much for that most elusive of treasures, success. When achieved, it is proudly, arrogantly and unabashedly displayed in the form of big houses, jewels, fancy cars, boats and airplanes. On the flip side, when calamity strikes, that proud and pompous peacock becomes a lame, half-blind goose, when his twelve-year-old daughter is diagnosed with cancer for which there is no cure. Now the money means nothing. The diamonds mean nothing. The house on the hill means nothing. The big boat in Miami won't help the broken heart heal, and the Rolls Royce won't make the trip to the cemetery any easier.

You people need to understand the gift of Creation, how rare and precious it is, and how long it took to get to this stage. Try not to squander it.

So many of you are stuck in your petty tribal, regional, political, ethnic, and religious differences that all but disappear, albeit briefly, when epic disasters strike. Earthquakes, floods, hurricanes, fires, volcanos, and tsunamis have an innate ability to bridge the chasm of hate and indifference, even if for a fleeting moment. When your crazy neighbor's house is burning, you are not reminded of the time he yelled at your kids, you are called to save and protect a precious life. A true calling, indeed.

"For someone who is so gruff and judgmental, you sure sound genuinely concerned about us. Am I sensing a caring attitude here?"

I may be judgmental, yes, but not gruff. And I have to maintain a certain set of character traits that enable me to do what I need to do. I have to be a realist. I screwed up the first Burst, and I have to make sure this one succeeds and forms a proper celestial expanding sphere, which in turn forces me to approach my many tasks different-ly than you might think. I cannot be individually selective in terms of who and what I support. We have to pay particular attention to humans and humanoids because you possess abilities which can become quite destructive to innocent species, possibly your whole world and even the Universe. Even though the Universe is vast, it is all inter-connected, and while her movements appear to be continuously outward, there is also a slight rota-tional component to it, which can in the distant future, present issues in some form of intergalactic contact. Such contact can produce undesired re-sults that can prove catastrophic for created life and set evolution back billions of years. I see the Universe progressing and maturing pretty much according to our expectations, and as the overseer, if you will, I want to see that continue. My concern for you derives from my desire to see you, human-oids, and all other living things, live life to the full-est, not just survive. All the while making sure you are not doing anything that harms nature and the animals. For those reasons, I have to remain neutral in my dealings with the various planets, their inhabitants and different tribes within those populations. To say life is rare in the Universe is to commit an understatement of monumental proportions, and because of its frailty, I have to be forever vigilant in its protection. Then again, at times it may become necessary to remove or modify life on some planet or galaxy knowing, that while that decision will save countless lives, it will also extinguish many others. This job is not easy. That Shakespeare guy had a good phrase for it. "Uneasy lies the head that wears a crown."

"You mean, 'Heavy is the head that wears a crown.'"

Again, you disappoint. Your grasp of Shakespeare is sadly lacking. Your version of that verse is a somewhat perverted one that is currently used by many, but I quoted the correct one. I'm assuming you understand it means that those in positions of authority and responsibility have a high burden placed upon them because of their station in existence. You would say "station in life" but the "life" part does not pertain to me, ergo, existence.

"Okay, I get it, but why are we talking about Shakespeare when I want to know about other planets and their inhabitants?"

As I have said before, all of the Universe is interconnected, and while you are unable to comprehend all its complexities, I am tasked with keeping the totality properly engaged and functioning. Got it?

"Actually, no, and please don't try to explain that last "totality properly engaged and functioning" part. I'm not sure my brain could take it right now. But do tell me about these more advanced planets."

The main one to talk about is 14-347. The other, 14-444, was also significantly more advanced than Earth but has suffered enormous geological upheaval which depleted 90% of the population over the last eight or nine thousand years. That planet, which is geologically very similar to your Earth, as is 14-347, had a colossal magma release which in turn released some poisonous gases thereby killing 90% of the trees and thus reducing the amount of available oxygen. Their population is down to fewer than two million, and it doesn't look like they will recover. From all reports I have seen, their oxygen levels have stabilized and may even be rising, but their plant life is having a tough time regenerating. Part of their problem is that they lost a significant amount of arable land plus the fact that planting trees requires manual labor to which they have not been accustomed for thousands of years. Their other major issue is a lack of pollinating insects, akin to your bees, which were all but destroyed during that catastrophe.

"If I may, it sounds like they could use your assistance."

> *Remember Moses? We are not going to be getting involved for the reasons I mentioned previously, and I am not sure that intervention on our part would have any significant impact within the time frame required. Hopefully they can glean knowledge from their history, resurrect ancient planting methods, and survive. It may be a tall order since, being so dependent on advanced technology, they are not accustomed to thinking in physical terms and concepts. Their world was essentially run by highly sophisticated machines controlled by, applying your standards, super intelligent beings. If I can phrase it in your terms, they outlived their humanness. They were some four hundred thousand years ahead of you developmentally but did not take care to maintain their physical development as well as their intellectual and mental capacities. Reliance on technology became the norm which morphed into an almost religious obsession, and all growth was concentrated on scientific advancements. The price was the degradation of the physical body to the point that beings who were once somewhat comparable to Earthenites in size, now resemble your children around the age of seven or eight but with much larger skulls and what appear to be shriveled limbs.*

Yes, conceptually, they are or were, very much like you and the beings on 14-167, and even though 14-167 is less advanced intellectually, they are physically very much like you. Standing upright, head, body, upper limbs, lower limbs, internal organs and a skeleton supporting it all, directed and controlled by a cranially enveloped brain. Actually, nature used this concept throughout the Universe, on most mammals and if you look carefully, the design concept is also present in most birds, with appropriate modifications, of course.

It appeared as if God had given up on the people before they were dead. I'm not sure how he was able to carry all that responsibility.

"Are they capable of reaching Earth? Do they have the space craft that can reach us?"

They did. But after the magma release, however, they stopped all extraterrestrial travel and concentrated on survival which is, understandably, their main point of being at this time. We visited rarely as they were great stewards of their planet and didn't need surveillance. The problem they are in now is beyond our ability to control and we are therefore staying away. I don't know if they ever visited Earth, but they did go to 14-347 often and cooperated jointly on other exploration of the Universe.

"You are telling me that you are just going to let them die, right?"

It is not within our ability to repair an individual planet. We have the capability to prevent galactic catastrophes, but not mend single planets. Those are the facts as we see them now. They may survive at their current population levels but will have to improve genetically if they are to endure as a species. They have the wherewithal, but the process is long and so are the odds. C'est la vie.

"But they still have the technology. Why don't they leave the planet? Go to 14-347?"

I'm sure some will do that and probably some already have. Vessels capable of traveling through the Universe are fairly small and can only transport a couple of dozen beings at a time plus the trip takes a number of years to complete. The math just isn't on their side.

From what I know, they are resigned to their fate and will work on the oxygen situation. You said yourself when we first started talking, you realized that all living things eventually die. This may very well be their time.

"Yes, I did say that. I just hadn't thought of it on a planetary level. We have a potential catastrophe just fourteen hundred miles from here. It's called Yellowstone, and we refer to it as a super volcano. Our geologists say that its eruption could kill more than half of Earth's population. Would you allow that to occur?"

I know about Yellowstone, and my latest information is that it last erupted about six hundred and forty thousand years ago. To the best of our knowledge, it is not due to erupt again for another one hundred and twenty thousand years, give or take five years, or so. And again, it is not within my purview to control individual planetary geological events. What will happen, will happen, but you are safe for the near term.

"Good to know, thanks. I can sleep easier now. Now let's talk more about the creation part. I can't stop thinking about it, okay?"

Okay.

"Let me just see if I have this right. You and the A's get all the matter together, imbue it with energy, and cause it to blow up. Do I have it right?"

Precisely.

"What happened after the Burst? How did the planets form? How does life happen?"

Those are two short questions which require long and somewhat complex answers. Do you have time? I know it's getting late, and don't you need to get your beauty rest?

"No, no. It's okay. Let's keep going. I know I'm not going to get another chance at this. Besides, I don't have to work for the next five days, so I can sleep tomorrow and the next day."

Okay. Pay attention, I'm not explaining this twice. You are not the only one on my schedule. After the Burst, basically all the matter turned into dust and was propelled out at immeasurable speed. That expansion took about five billion years to push all the dust out far enough so that gravitational coalescence could take place and the process of Universal consolidation could commence. I'm assuming that you know that these dust particles are not all the same size, and in time the smaller ones started to cling to the bigger ones and on and on and on, for a few billion years until we started to see big round shapes form into what you call celestial bodies. Some of these bodies consist of solid matter like rocks and water, some are gaseous, and some are basically pure energy. You call those stars, and we call them Lights of Life.

Gas also is not subject to gravitational attraction in the same way solid matter is, including water. It is held in place globally and that is what comprises an atmosphere and why you have air to breathe.

Some of the planets became solid, such as your Earth and Mars, and others became gaseous. Not all gas, just gaseous. Don't ask me to explain the gaseous part, it means nothing in this conversation. Since you have some brain function, you are aware that you cannot walk on gas, ergo, no life as you understand it on Jupiter and Saturn.

"You really like that word, ergo, don't you?"

Don't interrupt, I'm trying to teach you something. It's a perfect word for this context, and I use it for effect. Using "therefore" would be too banal.

Continuing.

As gravity continues to form all these celestial bodies, water, various gases, chemicals, and solids start to interact and, on planets that produced a conducive environment, life emerges. First it was a single-celled organism which turned into two and then four and so on. Eventually we got some little fish in the ocean to begin with, then bigger fish, and then some of them, disliking their neighbors start venturing onto the shore. In time they develop little legs, become amphibians and after a couple of billion years of evolution, here you are. In the interest of time, I am not going into all the details about how little fish evolved into bigger fish and how amphibians became land creatures, then grew fur, big teeth, muscles, aggressive tendencies, and arrogance. Now that I think about it, it seems like many with those traits morphed into lawyers. But again, I digress. All you need to know is that it happened, and as previously noted, we spread the seeds of life across the Universe, it took a long time for it to germinate, and the evolutionary journey is similar everywhere. But life only took hold on those planets where the conditions were right. Okay?

"Okay. Keep going."

No, that's enough for today. You go to bed now, and we'll continue in the morning. Besides the A's and I have to take a quick trip to Brazil. They are having a beach volleyball tournament and I hear the women are spectacular.

"Wait what? How does that work? Why would women interest you?"

> *Sometimes we commandeer human bodies to get the feeling of what it's like to be a life form. Sometimes we go as women, and sometimes we go as men and even animals. It's complicated, I'll explain it later, or maybe not. Goodnight.*

August 22, 2020

I woke up eagerly awaiting His return so we could continue our conversation, plus I was interested in that trip to Brazil. It was well past noon when I realized that He probably wasn't coming. So instead, I spent the better part of my day putting my notes from the last two days together, then went to sleep hoping He would return tomorrow.

August 23, 2020

Sure enough, at the stroke of six, He announced Himself.

> *Are you up? Okay, where did I leave off?*

I hadn't slept well, hadn't had any coffee yet, but I had to look sharp.

"I thought you were coming yesterday. What happened?"

I told you we were going to Brazil. We got side-tracked. That's all you need to know, besides you are not the boss of me.

"I see you are picking up some American teenager lingo."

I'm trying to relate. I've been told in the past that I can be overbearing and domineering.

"Overbearing? Domineering? You? Creator of the Universe. Why would anyone say that? What would possibly give someone that impression?"

Alright, wise ass. I'm trying to be nice to you and communicate on your level, and you mock me.

"I'm just trying to understand all this. Actually, just some of it, and you are belittling me."

Awww. Did I hurt your feelings?

"Look, I get it, you created all this, and you are proud of it. You screwed up the first attempt and you owned up to that. I really respect that. You didn't have to tell me that, and if you didn't, I would never have known. It's not like I can google 'First Big Bang Failure' and see what comes up. We thought we finally learned a little bit about all this and now you are telling me that we are not all that smart, and we need to evolve for hundreds of thousands of years more before we measure up to your standards. For your information, I am not an idiot. I have been a licensed architect for over forty years. Stick that in your cosmic energy pipe and smoke it."

I guess I struck a nerve, but facts are facts. You are not as advanced as others, and getting to their level takes time and evolvement. You kept bugging me all these years for a sit down, I finally show up, try to impart some knowledge, and you get upset?

"I'm not upset so much at you as I am disillusioned with the human race for all the reasons you point out. Wars, hatred, greed, politicians, lawyers, the IRS, and the fake preachers on TV who take advantage of poor gullible people. I always thought you could have done a better job of cleansing people of those shortcomings."

I understand, but those shortcomings are yours to overcome. When I first encountered beings such as you it took me thousands of years to figure out what we had done and why you turned out the way you did. Your kind is going through a civilizational upheaval that will separate the "wheat from the chaff," and while I may be tempted to bring celestial wrath upon you, I will not. You were provided a brain, and you must learn how to use it and what to do with it. You learned how to build grand structures, huge ships and airplanes, trains, dams, reversed river flows, dug canals that travel for miles and miles, burrowed into the Earth for minerals, oil and water. You harnessed the power of the atom, which I already mentioned. That could have waited a bit longer. You are walking on eggshells with that one, be careful. Many egos need to be tamed. While the task is enormous, you are definitely capable of accomplishing it. Just keep the lawyers out of the room. They always like to stick their noses into everything. Keeping politicians out will be impossible, but if you manage to include some statesmen and stateswomen, you will have a greater chance at success. By the way, just then I wasn't being condescending or trying my hand at political correctness, as you call it nowadays, with the stateswomen remark. Women do possess an innate protective mechanism that men can-not access, and this ability will be extremely valuable in forging the necessary common ground. When A5 directed nature to create you and the rest of the animals, you were both given that X chromosome, but without the other X chromosome, you just don't have the female intuition.

"You could have told me this forty years ago before I married the first one. Would have helped a lot. Speaking of women, did A5 really make one out a man's rib?"

Five minutes ago, I told you that you can't believe everything you read in books and now you ask me this? Because of that bullshit, people believe that men have fewer ribs than women. Go ahead, count them.

"Okay. 1, 2, 3, 4, 5, 6, 7, 8, 9, 10, 11, 12. Yep, 12 pairs. Now I have to find a woman and count hers."

Hah! That's funny, I'll give you that. Where are you going to find a woman who will let you count her ribs? Have you looked in the mirror lately? Not exactly triathlon material, you are. Believe me, they have 12 pairs also. Now and then you see someone with 11 or 13 pairs, but those people are anomalies. Just like people with six fingers on each hand.

"Low blow with the triathlon comment."

Just stating the obvious. You have looked better, admit it.

"Yeah, I know. You don't have to rub it in."

I just tell it like it is and how I see it. No sugarcoating and no lies. Truth and honesty are much easier to abide by, and you don't have to remember any of your lies. Now back to the rib thing.

Don't get me wrong, because there is an enormous amount of wisdom in the Bible, but much of it is also based on faith and a particular belief system where segments of society will divorce themselves from reality and common sense because of something written in a book allegedly inspired by God.

"It's like you read my mind. That was going to be one of my next questions. Wait, can you read my mind?"

Not like you can read a book, but I can feel and sense your soul. To me that is much more important. That's one reason I put you on the contact list during this trip.

"Oh! Wow. Let me digest that one for a bit. Thank you. Wait, I need to take a deep breath here."

I took a long sip of coffee hoping it would help my mind stop spinning. It didn't really, but I had to forge ahead.

"Anyway, how does one know what is true and what is not? Christians say one thing, Jews say another, and Muslims something else. Hindus, among other things, believe in reincarnation and the immortality of each soul. The followers of Shinto adhere to the belief that their kami or spirits, inhabit all living things. All appear to be well-meaning, but many members of each group are not so tolerant of others whose belief system is different from their own. Each of

these groups has within their own ranks members who ab-
hor even people within their own communities who simply
choose to eat different foods or wear what some consider
objectionable clothing. What's wrong with people?"

*As I see it, a lot of it is based on believers' inter-
pretations of the particular texts and thousands
of years of tradition. I personally avoid getting too
entangled in those, basically for the same reason
we, in general, don't interfere in local tribal in-
teraction. I mentioned my encounter with Moses
which taught me a valuable lesson, and since then
we will never pick sides in any local dispute, no
matter how brutal. There was a number of occa-
sions where we had opportunity to get involved
and even prevent deadly conflict but chose not to.*

"How do you manage to keep that distance? It has to be aw-
fully difficult."

*To repeat what I said earlier, if we help one side
and they perceive that we helped them due to
some of their own self-serving belief, we will render
that society devoid of self-reliance for thousands
of years. All beings, people, tribes, tribe members,
countries and planets have to work out all their
own conflicts between and among themselves.
Third party interference never results in a positive
outcome for all, and the aggrieved party always*

*blames the "peacemaker." Fix your own problems
people, that's why we gave you brains and the
ability to reason. How well you use that gift will
tell how you and subsequent generations prosper
in the future. Build that ever so vital foundation
for your progeny, and in time they will be grateful.*

*At the risk of sounding like an old hippie, love
more and hate less.*

"Amen to that. If only I could get some of my Earthenite
brethren to follow that simple edict, my life will not have
been for naught."

"Now that you have prepared me to cure most of mankind's
problems, I would like to get into a more esoteric subject.
Time."

What about it?

"Well, what is it, and when did it start? You've been men-
tioning it this whole time, no pun intended."

*Ooooh. You picked one of the good ones. First things
first. Time actually never started, and it does not
progress, it just is. Yes, I've heard the stories of it
starting at the instant of the Second Burst, your
Big Bang, and they are all preposterous. Who is
the genius that thought that one up? That would*

be something like a horse race or a hundred meter dash at the Olympics, where a guy stands there and fires this fake pistol into the air, and everybody takes off. The guy firing the pistol had to be there before the race started, to fire the pistol. Firing the pistol did not create the pistol or the guy. Just like there was preparation before the race, adjusting shoes, setting up the track, and such, there was preparation for the Burst, and I was the guy with the pistol. You get it? Obviously, there was a "before" prior to each event, ergo, we had time before each occurrence and "time" was an ongoing phenomenon, but only in the sense that there were living and finite elements present.

I managed to resist saying anything about the use of the word "ergo" . . . yet once more.

I look at it this way. Picture time as a gigantic Ferris wheel with an infinite number of seats and everyone gets into their pre-assigned seat at their prescribed time, travels the pre-destined distance and at the end of their journey they are released, and another passenger takes their place. This wheel was turning before anything was here and will continue to spin forever after all of it is no longer here again. Time is not the thing that moves. You and other living things move within it. It's not something you start, it's not something you stop, and it needs nothing to help it continue. It doesn't care if it's cold or if it's hot, night or day, it is just there and it keeps on turning. How's that for an explanation?

"Wow! Actually, when I was a kid, I had thoughts along those lines."

Sure you did.

"No, seriously. I was very curious as a kid. Except for the Ferris wheel thing. I envisioned it more like an infinite circular train composition onto which you are deposited at birth and dumped out at death, spiritually speaking."

Then, I suppose we agree to a point. Time is not something that can be measured. Your existence within it can be measured, which in essence says that if you don't exist, for you there is no time. At the instant of your conception, your time begins, somewhat akin to your own personal Big Bang, but whose duration is predictable. Hey, no wise cracks about the personal Big Bang. Taking it a step beyond the personal, at the moment of the Second Burst, the Universe's time, in its current state, began, but not everyone else's time. Those of us that existed prior to Creation continued on their time path and the ones in the dawn of their existence, embarked on their own time journey.

Until I told you, you did not know that we initiated the First Burst, recalled its expansion and cut short its duration due to Creator error. Did we stop time, or did we cut the length of the First Burst's existence? Is there a difference? Of course, there is. Then we endeavored to re-plan, re-engineer and re-assemble all the matter and energy into another attempt at Creation. During the re-assembly, did we stop time? No. All the original elements were still in existence but were now being halted in their flight and returned to the point of origin, for the second attempt. It's like you missing an exit on the highway on your way to your girlfriend Suzy's house and you're having to re-route. Nothing really changed except that you got to her house twenty minutes older than originally planned. And maybe you two missed the first game at the bingo parlor.

"Wait, you said you couldn't read my mind. How did you know my girlfriend's name was Suzy?"

Simple. It's been floating around in your soul off and on during this entire conversation. But that's not the point. The point is that your "scientists" are not at the level required to probe into the Universe's past far enough, to provide answers to questions you still don't know you need to ask. To be fair, they are still learning and finding things that are still unexpected, and the quest for that learning will provide many, not all, answers they seek.

"Let me get this straight. If there is nothing alive, time essentially does not exist. Did I phrase that correctly? "

You are close. Everything is affected during the period of its existence, and not just what you perceive as living objects. We all know the simple stuff: grass, trees, birds, mice, dogs, lions, fish, monkeys, people, and all the other animals and plants. Those things that you consider as inanimate, such as rocks, water, or soil also are passengers on that train of yours. Their time on your train is much longer than that of living things mentioned earlier but you are still connected to them by your mutual presence on that train. Stated a different way, you are inseparably connected to them, because, without them you cannot exist, yet, without you they would do just fine and in fact would fare better, given how poorly you have treated them with your air, sea, and land pollution. If there is nothing or nobody on the train, there is no time effect, and at that particular place and time, time does not exist. However, the instant an object manages to get a seat on the train, time is activated for that object.

With all this talk of time, my mind felt like I was spinning on a never ending Ferris wheel at the moment.

"This is getting really deep and intense. Can we have a moment of levity? Why don't you tell me about your trip to Brazil and how the whole concept of you ogling women works?"

> *Ah, I see. Back to Brazil. In a nutshell, we, the A's and I, can increase our presence in a human, from our normal and natural levels, and be able to see and feel what you see and feel.*

"How do you do that? Better yet, what exactly are you? I know who you are, but what are you? I can't see you, I don't hear you, and I obviously can't touch you. All I can do is sense you. How is it that I can sense you, and how is it that I understand everything you are 'saying?'"

> *Finally. I would have thought that question would have been at the top of your list. Why didn't you ask that at the outset of this encounter?*

"Well, at first, I thought it was all a dream and since I've never had a dream like this, I didn't want it to end and was somewhat reluctant and, frankly, scared. I'm assuming very few people have gone through something like this, and let me tell you, it's not easy to comprehend. I keep waiting for the other shoe to drop and somebody to come running out yelling 'April fools.' Then I realize that it's August, and a myriad thoughts and questions go through my mind. Again, what are you?"

> *That is another short question with a long answer. We are eight. I am the first and I am the Creator of the Plan. The other seven help me implement the Plan. Each of us is responsible for our individual developments, and together we manage the expansion and all that it entails. We are not beings, we are not guardians, we are not spirits, and we are not angels. The reason I refer to them as angels is to make it easier for you to understand since you have been hearing that term for millennia. We are energy. We are eight clusters of energy, and we are an integral part of all that we created. I am the creator of this planet, and billions like it, and I am in every molecule of water and every cell of every living thing on this planet you call Earth, as well as on all the other living planets. Actually, what was created is a lot more than just the planets. The Second Burst put into motion an accumulation of conditions that produced all the elements necessary for life, and when they coalesced into what you call Earth, your life began. This planetary coalescence also took place in a number of other locations, mainly in the fourteenth quadrant, as I mentioned earlier. There doesn't appear to be any rhyme or reason for a planet's advanced or delayed growth. The more I think about it, the*

more it looks like a grand lottery. It appears to be the product of when and how quickly life's basic elements managed to consolidate on a planet that possessed all the other of life's prerequisites. Location to its master star was extremely important in the creation of climate, and the planet's size was also key. Too small and the creatures, by definition have to be tiny, too big and you have a gaggle of giants of all species, which would require extreme amounts of food which the planet could not produce.

When all of that is compiled and you start to think how precious and rare of a gift you possess, it boggles the mind to think that one of mankind's greatest ambitions is to destroy itself. For what? He is white, she is black, and that other one yellow? And that one over there is red. Red? Yellow? Then there are the hairy ones and the bald ones and the tall ones and the short ones, skinny ones and fat ones, smart ones and the less than smart ones. Don't forget the brown ones and the beige ones, can't leave them out. They have more of what we want, so we should go get it. What if they don't let us? That's a problem. Oh, damn, we've been down this road before, and all those roads are paved with death. Jericho, Arbela, Tours, Hastings, Orleans, Kosovo, Vienna, Yorktown, Waterloo, Gettysburg,

Stalingrad, Normandy, Pearl Harbor, Hiroshima and on and on and on and on. Where does it end?

I'm sorry, I went off topic there, but you just don't stop. You people have to learn sometime.

"I understand what you are saying, but we can't be the only planet with this kind of insanity. What about the other ones? Have they been able to avoid cataclysmic conflicts?"

Most have, but not without great difficulty and one paid dearly. More on that subject later.

"Okay, let me get to something that's been gnawing at me all this time. How is it that I hear you but there is no sound?"

This is how the A's and I communicate across the cosmos, and I have simply added you to our circle. You notice that most of the time you are not speaking either, just projecting thoughts, and I answer in kind. You will have to go back to the system of communication you are accustomed to as soon as I leave.

"I'm trying to comprehend, but it is not that easy. When you first contacted me a couple of days ago, you said you didn't know where I was or whether it was day or night. Where exactly were you at the time? Where are you now?"

I'm not exactly sure, but somewhere in the Milky Way. Since part of me is in every living thing, I am therefore connected to all living things at once. Think of me as a cosmic shadow that covers about ten percent of Creation. As I move around, I don't really depart from one particular place for quite some time. I have a center of sorts, not unlike an animal or human brain, from which I sense all that surrounds me, but I cannot "see" where individuals may be. That's why I said that I had no idea where you were and what time it was. Besides, as we discussed a little bit ago, time is a bit more complex than you Earthenites think. Now let me get back to how the little fish became the big fish story.

"The ones that wanted to be amphibians?"

Yes those. Now listen. Those snobby fish that didn't like being wet all the time ventured onto the shore and over many millions of years developed propulsion limbs to provide them movement abilities on land. These propulsion limbs eventually turned from flippers into legs and arms in many animals, including primates and you guys. Actually, you are primates, just a little bit more cunning than the rest of your cousins. They forage for food and seek shelter from predators and the elements, while you covet things that don't belong to you. If you want to see what you looked like in the beginning of your evolutionary journey, go find a salamander and study it closely. For some reason they liked it in the water and decided to forego the evolutionary process and remained in the water.

That is likely what you looked like ninety or so million generations ago. If you look closely, you may recognize Uncle Sal's lazy eye in one of them.

"Yeah, he's really sensitive about his lazy eye."

I know. But that's not the point. The point is that all this is happening over millions of years, eventually evolving into you, an imperfect animal who needs to develop further and has much to learn about the gift he was given. I know, I know, he or she, was given. Before you ask, humans did not evolve from monkeys, but you do seem to have some common ancestry evidenced by nearly identical DNA between you and chimpanzees. I'm not exactly sure when, but just like those snobby fish, one of your tree-dwelling ancestors didn't like exerting himself by swinging through the trees and decided he would rather go walking in the moonlight than swinging from branch to branch. That was the birth of true snobbism, as the "Walkers" that's what they called themselves started looking down their protruding noses at their flat-nosed cousins. On the other hand, the "Chimps," as they still call themselves, maintain their ability to grasp items such as tree limbs, little kids' sandwiches and women's purses at zoos, with both their feet and their hands. Their constant knock on the Walkers was and continues to be, "You would be a better thief if you could grab with both your feet and your hands." To which the Walkers always replied, "Don't worry about us, we have lawyers for that while the best you can do is throw crap at visitors." Realizing this truth is the main reason that every time you see chimps at the zoo, they have that sad look in their eyes. Once in a while you can even hear them whisper, "If I had flat feet, I could have been somebody. I could have been a contender."

I hope that is sufficient for now. You really don't need all the details about the emergence of life since the outcome would still be the same. Besides, if I went into that much minutia, it would be tantamount to asking a politician what time it was and as usual, he would proceed to tell you how a watch is made . . . or at least try to make you believe he knew how a watch was made.

"Wait, how can these salamander things forego the evolutionary process? It isn't like somebody took a salamander census and asked who wanted to remain a wannabe waterborne-rat and who wanted to go on to bigger and better things."

> *Again, you astound me with the extent of your evolutionary knowledge. You are correct, there was no census. The census takers went on strike about a couple thousand years before the salamandarian exodus mainly because the salamanders were quite uncooperative and constantly lied about the number of inhabitants in their water abodes and were always splashing water on the census forms making them unreadable. The cosmological Director of Evolution paid the salamanders a visit one day and gave them an ultimatum to either complete the formwork as required or to de-register and remove themselves from the evolutionary path. Not being fond of cosmic bureaucratic threats, salamanders told him what he could do with his formwork and promptly filed for de-registration from the Future Terrestrial Association, better known in those days as, FTA.*

> *That allowed those in your DNA soup to maintain their evolutionary course and eventually produce cats, lions, giraffes, elephants, primates, and the likes of you.*

I knew God was joking, at least about part of it. But I still wrote it all down.

"Going back to that lazy chimp ancestor. I didn't know that we actually evolved out of laziness."

> *Not laziness. Your profound arrogance. You thought and still do, that you are the stewards of this planet and have "dominion" over nature and the animals. Yes, I know that the Bible states that man should have this dominion, but again, you can't believe everything you read in books. Authors take liberties all the time.*

"Wait, who wrote the Bible?"

> *Even your scholars don't agree on the origins and authors of the Bible. Some say that Moses wrote parts of it, some say that Jesus wrote parts of it, some say it was written by a whole bunch of guys over many centuries. Still others say that many priests stuck in a few paragraphs here and there. Nobody knows for sure since there is no original to compare all your current versions to. I've even heard that some parts were written by women but those were tossed or hidden.*

> *Then there are those who say that most people of that time, including Moses and Jesus, were illiterate, begging the question, how could they write anything? I suppose they could have dictated their*

texts to some scribe, which in turn begs another question. How would the "writer" know what the scribe was writing? The guy could say "Goliath was this warrior and David met him on the battlefield and following a horrific fight, slew him" but the scribe, thinking the notion of Goliath being ordinary would not sell well, embellished it a bit by making him a youthful giant and blessing David with profound slingshot skills. On top of which he instills in David extraordinary bravery by refusing the armor Saul offered him. See? That made a much better story and put that book on the all-time bestseller list.

Getting back to the notion of dominion. Your arrogance is just astounding. Don't get offended, by you, I mean you Earthenites, not you, personally. Some guy, from God knows when, writes in a book saying that man should have dominion over nature and animals, and you take it at face value. You people can't even clean snow off the streets in the wintertime, but you want dominion. Let me tell you a little bit about nature. A5, my animal creative director, took millions of years to develop animals that can walk, run, fly, swim, communicate, hunt, and reproduce. Just how would you assume dominion over that lot?

I can just imagine what a fiasco it would be if your kind had the task of creating animals and devising their behavior, their reality, and their survival.

How would you go about teaching lions to behave or explaining to elephants where they can or cannot go? I'd love to see that. Six guys sitting in a "board room" proposing an agenda for coming up with a procreating protocol for tigers. Or how about instilling horses, better yet, cats, with the ability to swim?

It took the eight of us over a million years just to develop the concept of an eye, then another two, to actually construct one that would function properly and form the basis for evolution to expand on and perfect into what animals use today. I can just see those board room guys "brainstorming" about what needs to be included in "eye design" and setting parameters to be handed off to the engineers to figure out.

That would have been just perfect. One eye on top of the head or worse yet, to one side, forcing you to walk sideways with a perennial crick in your neck.

When you people invented the street signal light it took two years of discussion on whether the red or green light should be on top. And you thought you were given dominion of the animals because someone wrote it in a book thousands of years ago? You were going to take care of the animals? You can't take care of yourselves, and you thought you could care for nature's creatures? Don't make me laugh.

Look at the garbage in the ocean which is killing my fish, and you want dominion? As I said, you can't believe everything you read in books. Especially books written many centuries ago by unknown people making up their own facts as they saw fit. In those days people didn't know any better and were essentially told what to believe, and they believed it.

And yes, I know there is some tiny bug with only one eye not two, and A5 said it was because the bug was so small, there was no room for two. I wondered why he made a bug that small to begin with but didn't say anything because I didn't want to hurt his feelings. He's made enough blunders in his animal development program that we had to step in and get rid of some of his species. I really shouldn't be so hard on him. Creating flora is exceptionally difficult, but creating fauna is a monumental task.

Many tiny details had to be developed, tested, and perfected before they could be placed into production. For example, in the beginning, we started with small creatures that had only four senses. Sound, smell, touch, and taste. We never even considered something called sight. They lived in caves and deep bodies of water where there was nothing to see due to absence of light. Besides, we can't see, and we are doing okay. But then, as they started coming out of the caves and deep water, that's where the whole eye thing came up.

Anyway, where was I? Oh right.

So, as bigger and more complex creatures arrived, I realized that sight would be useful. Imagine a dinosaur, mammoth, giraffe, or elephant trying to get around by just using touch, smell, and sound. Finding food would be almost impossible, and they would go extinct before they had a chance to exist. So, as I said earlier, sight was developed. Since I "see" using my Creator's sense, which is only present in those of us that were here prior to the First Burst, it was very difficult to envision, no pun here, how sight would work. Creating the Universe was easier. We just blew stuff up, all the dust started to coalesce, at some point we triggered gravity and viola we had a galaxy, then another and another and then, life.

I am probably repeating myself here but given the amount of material I have to cover here, it should not be surprising.

"I gotta say I'm in real deep water here. I know, sixty-five years of asking, but I never expected this. Nobody said you would come knocking and actually talk to me, so forgive me if I'm a little uncertain about all this. You are telling me about a failed attempt at Creation, other living planets, other beings, a planet dying, interplanetary travel, and how we aren't smart and are not developed enough. It's all a bit too much to digest at one time."

Take solace, my Earthenite friend, your group is not the dumbest one in the Universe. We have some that are far worse where we have even decided to plant a few shills among their lot to see if we can point them in the right direction.

"I thought you and the A's didn't interfere."

That's true in most cases, but these people were using up their natural resources way too fast and they had to slow down. So, we planted a few of our brighter folks who "invented" new methods of resource management, and the problem was solved without anybody knowing we had a hand in it.

"So, there is some empathy in you, after all."

Yes, but on a case-by-case basis.

"Okay, I get it. Let me get back to the Universe if I may?"

Sure.

"I just want to get this straight because of what I was taught most of my life. I found it difficult to believe that you as the Creator of our Universe, were not aware of what was happening in it at all times, but now that you've explained the magnitude of it all, it is becoming clearer."

Not sure who taught you that in the first place, but the way you're thinking now is correct. Listen carefully, I'm about to reveal to you a lot of truths, and I hope you are capable of understanding it all. Number one, don't call it our Universe. You are less than a millionth of a grain of sand in the whole scheme of things and have no standing in the ownership of any part of it. Again, it is my Universe. There was a scientist on Earth some time ago, Carl Sagan, who is associated with the phrase, "billions and billions of galaxies." Actually, it was that TV guy, Johnny Carson, who coined the phrase after Sagan's many visits to the Tonight Show. I digress. What Sagan was saying is that there indeed are billions and billions of galaxies that comprise the Creation, but as smart as he was, he didn't know about the seven sectors. By the way, he too, was married three times like you, so there may be hope for you after all. Pay attention. Try to imagine billions and billions multiplied seven times. Don't try using your computer to calculate the number, it doesn't have the capability of computing a number that big. Among all those billions and billions, there are only five planets that currently have sentient, thinking, reasoning humanoid life, and then try to imagine how rare and therefore precious, that life is. For some reason they all happen to be the fourteenth quadrant.

What you were taught to believe is not something that I control, encourage or have any input on, whatsoever. I worked relentlessly to create a situation where you would come to be, evolve, learn, and prosper. So far, what humanity has been able to accomplish well is the development of horrific weapons of war. Your advancements in medicine, engineering, mathematics, physics, and chemistry are admirable but still far short of what is possible. I mentioned previously that I wished you humans would increase your brain cell usage, but I realized that evolution is something that cannot be hurried, and I guess I will just have to wait.

"If you are the Father and Creator of all, why would you allow us to continue on this path of destruction?"

I try and I try, but you don't listen. And who told you I was your Father? I am not anybody's Father. I am the Creator of the Universe, and I am in the process of promoting and advancing life as much as possible, but that process is long and tedious. I didn't put you on the path to destruction. That was your own doing and therefore, by definition, I had no role in "allowing" you to continue on any path. What the eight of us did was create the segments that make up the Universe, seed those segments with elements necessary for life to exist and then monitor life development as it started to blossom. We watched as the first organisms expanded to multicellular ones, and after a few billion years, we wound up with you. I've seen the claim that this was done in six days, but one thing was not explained in those books. My day is about seven hundred million Earth years long. The reason I keep saying Earth years is that years on other planets are of different duration. On planet 14-347, the "year" is approximately twice as long as on Earth. The climate is similar, but the seasons are twice as long since it takes twice as long to go around their sun. In case you were wondering, their sun is further away from the planets, hence the longer trip. Their sun is also hotter than the Earth's sun, thus the similarity in climates.

The little bits and pieces of what He was saying were finally starting to come together.

"So, you are not the being from the Holy texts who created Adam, Eve, the serpent and the Devil. You are one of eight Creators of the Universe, and you happen to be the Leader. Do I have this part right?"

Yes, you are correct. Your holy texts were written by "learned" men trying to explain the unexplainable but were just not scientifically advanced enough. They based everything on the concept of belief, and they told the people what to believe. Look at what those learned men did to Galileo. He figured out the Earth revolves around your Sun, and they almost crucified him. Many at that time thought the Earth was flat and if you sailed too far west you would fall off. Amazingly, some "people" still think the Earth is flat. You really have to wonder what they are smoking.

Anyway, not my problem. I gave you brains and the ability to use them. How you use them is up to you. You have evolved enough to understand that working and living together in a cooperative spirit is preferred to living in constant strife and conflict, but you often have leaders who prefer friction and animosity in order to maintain power. Obviously, some of those leaders are imposed upon you by force whereupon people have to rise up and take control back from the tyrants. This involves more conflict and slows down the process of evolution which is needed for mutually beneficial advancement. We have two other life planets, 14-347 and 14-444, that had similar problems but managed to overcome them and thrived way beyond your capabilities to understand. That's not a slight on your intelligence, just a big plus for theirs. This is a concept similar to aging where the "older you" realizes how stupid the "younger you" was. Your evolution will accelerate much faster when you learn this simple notion and teach your younger generations to thirst for knowledge and wisdom and not burden themselves with designer jeans, Louis Vuitton purses, cars du jour, and the wide array of electronic trinkets and games promoted by the vast Fifth Avenue Empire. If they, from an early age, understand that with all oars rowing the same direction, the desired destination is reached much faster, and the trip will have been much smoother. Of course, you will have to explain what oars are, to many of your younger tribe members, if you can get them away from their Call of Duty, Super Mario, Minecraft, the latest version of Doom or the vast array of other mind-numbing game offerings from your electronic overlords.

"I find it fascinating that you are knowledgeable about video games. How do you know about all these fashion items and current tech?"

I said I wasn't all knowing, but I didn't say I was an idiot either. In order to know what is going on and especially on my life planets, I have to know what my inhabitants are doing and what direction they are traveling in. If one of my life planets becomes too overconfident and aggressive, I am obligated to investigate and, if necessary, address the situation. That may require a myriad of adjustments that would not be discernable by said inhabitants but would eventually reduce stresses on that neighborhood. Can't have planets invading other planets, simply put. It hasn't happened yet and as long as I'm the boss, it will not happen.

"Would that not be considered interference?"

Yes and no. And as always, we have to walk that fine line. Our primary goal is to protect life as much as possible, and for now we just have to monitor the more developed planets. The only more advanced planets are in your segment 4, quadrant 14. Remember from our earlier conversation, there are seven segments each with four quadrants each. Segment 1 has quadrants 1 through 4, segment 2 has quadrants 5 through 8, segment 3 has quadrants 9 through 12, segment 4 has quadrants 13 through 16, and so on. When you think about it, it makes perfect sense that there are various levels of development out there. Not only does the planet have to become mature enough to support life by providing the necessary elements needed, but the inhabitants have to evolve to partake of the gift. Mind you, we did not intend for humanoids such as yourself to evolve. We were perfectly content with the animals A5 created but then he went a little off-book and came up with dinosaurs, saber tooth tigers, and some nasty pigs the size of cows with six-inch-long teeth and worse.

No part of that development can be put on schedule because of the myriad steps it took for your own evolution. On 14-490, for instance, their humanoid beings are approximately two hundred thousand Earth years behind you. They are walking upright, have some primitive tools, and still live in caves. As I said earlier, each sector has three or four planets with life, and these vary widely in their development. A few dozen planets out there have primitive life that at some point may evolve into something more complex, but that's a long way off. When I say long way off, I mean millions of years off, not something that we'll see soon. Primitive life here means approximately a thousand evolutionary events before your glorious salamander.

On the other end of the evolutionary scale, we have 14-347, with their extraordinary achievements. They have solved their energy issues and are very adept at space travel.

"Hold up, hold up. How did they solve their energy issues? Solar, wind, nuclear, what?"

That's all you morons think about. You have all the energy you will ever need right under your feet and just a tiny bit is utilized. Geothermal. All of it is available free, courtesy of yours truly and nature, but you people are pushing sources that are not consistent and always at the whim of the weather. When it's cloudy, solar doesn't do much, when it's not windy, turbines don't produce much electricity, yet your genius politicians keep promoting solar and wind. Why would they do that? Makes you wonder, doesn't it? In a nutshell, 14-347 has a series of tunnels that took a few hundred years to construct, deep enough to collect the heat from the core. Heat is utilized in two ways, heated liquid is pumped to heating distribution plants and hot air is released through vertical channels to allow the rising air movement to spin turbines which in turn produce electricity. Again, this took hundreds of years to develop and construct and took the cooperation of all inhabitants. That's why they don't have serious conflicts and certainly no wars and continue to prosper and maintain the necessary balance to keep the planet healthy and vibrant. They realized that they had a common enemy, disappearing fossil resources, banded together and solved the problem. Once you reason using common sense, the toughest problems become mere challenges that are solvable.

While the concept is simple, you people are most likely not developed enough to understand its simplicity because the most important component is cooperation among the tribes. Unfortunately, that is still something you need to learn and master.

Also stop interrupting and let me finish my train of thought.

"I'm sorry, I was just curious."

Be quiet and let me continue. The inhabitants of 14-347, don't venture too far from their planet anymore, having realized that there is no place like home, plus the cost is way off the scale.

Essentially there is no return on investment, and at some point, there is no more money.

Interestingly enough, I heard that some of your wealthier inhabitants have their sights set on providing trips to "outer" space in the very near future and even colonizing Mars at some point. When I heard that, I almost fell over laughing, so to speak. Colonize Mars? This from people who still take five hours to issue a driver's license. Just for starters, Mars has no oxygen to speak of, which means you would have to bring your own. They'll need a big tank. Next on the list is the fact that Martian soil cannot support plant growth, ergo, no food. Another big tank. Bringing animals is another challenge that would be almost impossible to achieve, since they require the same conditions as you geniuses. To top it all off, Mars has only briny water which will have to be cleansed and made potable. More big tanks.

Maybe all that money should be spent on curing hunger and diseases among your less fortunate brethren. Cleaning up the oceans would also be another step in the right direction.

There was some talk of that Martian venture being a way of saving the human species in case of some catastrophic calamity on Earth. Being immensely arrogant as you are, you again are assuming that you are worth saving. Instead of spending those resources cleaning up your current and past screw-ups, you want to go to another planet and continue the process there. Besides, how many people could they take to make a difference? Now, for the big question. Who would get to go to this new paradise? Joe and Anne Marie Six Pack from Brooklyn or Biff and Buffy Harrington from the Hamptons?

That would be precious. Who would fix Biff's oxygen tank when it started to act up? Hang in there Biffy, we are sending someone over. He'll be there in about eight months and part of your charges will be his travel time to the job and back to our shop. The service call fee will be $5.58 billion plus 68 million miles at $17.89 per mile travel time for a total of $6.796 billion. Which credit card would you like to use?

Obviously, a perfect plan.

"Couldn't agree more. Yeah, we do have some problems here on Earth. From what I've read, eight million pieces of plastic find their way into our oceans every day, and one hundred million marine animals die from plastic each year. But colonize another planet? It's all ego."

If there's a question in there, you just answered it yourself.

"Yeah, I guess I did. So let me get back to the space travelers. I've been dying to ask this question for two days now. Have the guys from 14-347 visited Earth?"

Yes, they have. If I'm not mistaken, they are the ones some of your people call the grays due to their appearance. They are short in stature, large head compared to yours, and small bodies with skinny arms and legs. Very similar to the folks from 14-444 and pretty much for the same reasons. They appear to be looking to improve their genetic makeup and are trying to see if there is some compatibility with you creatures so they can create a shortcut to "reverse" the evolutionary process needed to bring back some of their lost physical attributes. While they are exceptionally intelligent, they have neglected their physical upkeep, much like the beings on 14-444 and want to prevent the same fate befalling them, should they be faced with something similar.

"So, you are telling me that inhabitants from 14-347 have the actually visited Earth?"

Were you not listening? I just said so.

"I was, I was, it's just not that simple to digest. Little gray men, flying saucers, aliens, extraterrestrials, even though I've heard about all this before, it still isn't easy to believe. How do they travel all that distance, what do they eat on the way, how long does it take, what kind of propulsion do they employ? Why are those things saucer-shaped, anyway?"

Well, you are at least asking the right questions. Don't get excited, those questions don't put you ahead of the class, so don't go patting yourself on the back. Millions have asked the same things before you.

Do a little exercise. Go back in history a couple of hundred years and research what technologies were available at that time. Look at the phones, typewriters, electric washing machines, cars, trains, and airplanes. Phones were invented around 1876, typewriters 1867, electric washing machines 1916, cars 1886, trains 1804, and the plane in 1903. Now compare those first inventions to today's models. Phones, you carry in your pocket. Typewriters are pretty much on their way out, although some manufacturers remain. Washing machines can be programmed to do almost anything you need to achieve cleanliness. Trains reach speeds upward of 300 miles per hour and some planes can go over Mach 3. In case you can't keep up with the math, that is over 2,000 mph. The first flight flown by your Wright Brothers flew for 12 seconds and covered 120 feet. In a little over 115 years the airplane went from 12 seconds in the air to 2,000 mph. Now, use today as the zero mark and project out 100 years into the future. Almost scary if you interpolate from your history. And now, for the big idea. What if one of my planets is hundreds of thousands of years ahead of your Earth as Michio Kaku said? I know what their advancements are but trying to explain them to you will be somewhat difficult. Actually, explaining won't be that difficult. Getting you to comprehend would be the tough part.

"I know I'm not what is referred to as the sharpest knife in the drawer, but as you so eloquently stated about your abilities, I'm not an idiot either. Give it your best shot."

Fine. Let's start with the saucer shape. As I understand it, it is derived from the fact that the craft is multi directional and does not need air and speed to create lift as in your airplanes. The propulsion system is based on harnessing and storing energy from the surrounding celestial bodies. I'm sure you people will figure it out some day.

In any case, they have had flying aircraft for well over 395 thousand years and have been exploring space around them for about 390 thousand years.

They have solved the distance issue by using something way beyond your capacity to comprehend. The propulsion used is called Shadow Flight, and essentially it is a smaller and much milder version of what the A's and I utilize. What they do is project an energy net along their path, extract energy from every available source on that path, and use that energy, in essence, to slingshot their way along the planned route. It provides speeds in excess of the speed of light and requires no input from the crew until arrival at the desired destination. Are you with me, Einstein?

"Again, you mock, but that's okay, this stuff is fascinating. How long is the trip from 14-347 to here?"

From 14-347 to 14-297 is about 30 Earth years. 14-297 is Earth in case you don't remember. While en route, the crew is placed in a type of hibernation which slows down their heart rates to about ten to twelve beats per hour, just enough to keep the lungs and brain oxygenated and keeps their aging down to less than one half of one percent of normal. When you publish the account of our encounter, make sure your "scientists" are made aware of these two crucial pieces of the space travel puzzle. That is, of course, if they manage to master that Shadow Flight thingy and are able to construct a craft that will withstand the rigors of such an undertaking. Just between you and me, the Shadow Flight took approximately eight thousand years to develop and another two thousand to perfect and these folks were developmentally, at least, one hundred thousand years beyond you when they began developing the concept. The long and short of it is, it isn't coming soon to an airfield near you. Then you have to go and find volunteers who are willing to leave their loved ones for sixty years on a mission that may end in failure, which in their case would obviously mean death, since there is no AAA out there in the perpetual darkness._

"Then why would they attempt such a journey?"

I told you. They were looking for a genetic shortcut to repair their depleted DNA, and as with you Earthenites, they developed a very healthy sense of self-importance as they too, thought themselves far superior to all others. There was, of course, a great deal of validity to that claim demonstrated by their many achievements. They eventually realized that there is a cost to such arrogance when they were again reminded of their frailty when 14-444 experienced their downfall. We maintained our distance as usual and watched from the sidelines knowing that sooner or later reason *and common sense would win over arrogance, with a little push from Mother Nature. No matter what any of you do, never forget that Nature will always protect herself, which means that if you do not pay her the proper respect, respect will be collected on your way out. Just like the IRS, no getting around it.*

"Depleted DNA? And that was from too much reliance on technology?"

They concentrated on their intellectual and mental capacities and neglected their physical bodies. While their intellectual powers grew exponentially, their bodies diminished in size to half of what they were at the beginning.

"I'm surprised that with all that intellect they didn't catch on sooner what was happening to them, and they now have to chase all over the Universe to find a remedy. I also heard that there are people who claimed to have been abducted by aliens who performed medical procedures on them. Most, if not all, those claims were debunked and or dismissed for one reason or another. Do you know if they achieved any results from those missions?"

I see that some of what I'm telling you is getting through since you don't show any skepticism about their ability to travel here from their planet. I'm

glad that my "teachings" are having an effect. It
gives me hope that you are on the right path.

"Thank you. I look at it this way. You can tell me whatever you want, and, in most instances, I would have no way of checking the validity of your information, and you know that. Then I look at the fact that you took over sixty-five years to contact me and by that fact alone, I cannot fathom what benefit you would derive from lying to me. Also, you said that you don't lie, and I'm choosing to believe you."

Wow! Just when I think that you are average, you surprise me. You are absolutely correct. I have no reason or benefit to feed you lies. What I would like to do is point out some of the downfalls your kind faces and perhaps enlist your help in averting some of them.

First, you need to take care of your environment, namely air and water pollution. Second, put massive armaments on the back burner. When crops fail, guns are useless. Finally, start talking to each other, not at each other. And take politics out of science.

"Is that all? That's a pretty tall order for an old man without an extended 'platform' from which to deliver the message without sounding like a nut. Besides, well-seasoned folks like me are not considered 'in' these days, and we tend to get easily dismissed."

Give it your best shot. I'm sure someone will listen.

"Surely you understand what a monumental task that is. Especially for a lone voice in today's world where everyone is out for themselves, and the loudest fools are the ones controlling the narrative. But I will try."

Write a book on it. Maybe it will be a bestseller. I know there are many people hungry for normality, and many great things were started by a single voice. Besides, if you don't try, you will never know.

"Thank you for believing in my abilities, that means a lot. Nonetheless, the task is still a lot to take on. Anyway, getting back to travelers from 14-347, are they still coming here?"

Not really. They have some craft that have been out for some time and most likely will never return mainly because they have no family to return to and have no applicable results to bring back. Eventually, they will just drift off into the darkness and disappear.

"That means their quest for DNA didn't work out?"

Apparently not.

"That's too bad and what a crappy way to go."

I know, but there are not too many pretty stories out there. What else do you have for me?

"You mentioned earlier that you had to get rid of some undesirable species that A5 created. Which ones?"

When we realized that evolution on Earth was eventually going to produce humanoid type creatures as it did on other planets, we knew we had to rid your planet of dinosaurs. There was no way for you guys to coexist with those things. They were just too big and too ferocious for you to survive. Getting rid of them was another affair I don't care to repeat.

"You got lucky with that meteor, right?"

It was an asteroid, and luck had nothing to do with it. We set out to find the best way of accomplishing the task without killing all life. It was decided that we would bring an asteroid into Earth's gravitational pull and once there, direct it to the optimal impact point. The search took some fifty thousand years because we had to make sure the asteroid was big enough to cause catastrophic damage to major species, namely dinosaurs, but

leave enough others to allow evolution to contin-
ue, and it had to be small enough not to break the
planet apart.

"The planet breaking apart was a possibility?"

Sure, and it still is, but the risk now is greatly di-
minished because we have a ring of black holes
positioned in a way such that errant and poten-
tially planet destroying celestial objects can be
deflected away from Earth and the other four
life planets. You guys still have to learn how that
works, but just know that we are out there looking
out for you. And while technically this was inter-
ference, it was not taking sides of one tribe against
another. We were protecting creatures that were
important to us.

So, this dinosaur asteroid . . . once it was iden-
tified and brought near Earth, A4 had to make
preparations for impact for which there could be
no rehearsals. Once it was released, it had to land
exactly in its predetermined spot or it was going
to be lights out for everyone. It all worked out. Di-
nosaurs went extinct in about eight hundred fifty
thousand years, and we have birds as remnants of
those monsters. As you can see, this creation stuff
takes a lot of work and constant diligence to main-
tain the promise and majesty of life.

"Why couldn't you get rid of the rats at the same time?"

> *Too many, just too damn many, and their gestation period is only about twenty-four days. Besides, evolution on other planets taught us that some of them morphed and evolved into higher mammals and ultimately primates. Since we didn't know which ones were destined for that journey, we let them all go on.*

"Listen, we covered a great amount of material and I need to transcribe before it gets too cumbersome. If you have no objection, I would like to do that and continue in the morning."

> *Whatever you say, champ. I'll be here at 7:00 sharp, be ready.*

August 24, 2020

> *Let's go, up and at 'em. Your new best friend, the Creator, is here.*

"I am here and I'm ready. I've had my coffee, breakfast and have yesterday's conversation all documented. I've also organized more questions to ask."

> *Then let's hear them.*

"Great. First question of the day. Earlier you mentioned that you are part of every living thing out there. How exactly does that work?"

> *Good one, I'm glad you are paying attention and not asking for favors like winning the lottery or something. Previously I told you that I am a cluster of energy but more accurately, I am an array of energy that stretches across Creation with particular concentration on the living planets. Since those are physically very distant from one another, my presence is commensurate with the area I cover so I can be in somewhat close proximity if needed. At any one time, I can cover approximately eighty percent of the fourteenth quadrant. So much for real estate.*
>
> *This next part is important so pay close attention. Every time a human-like creature is born it is consigned a sliver of my energy and a lifetime connection is formed. Other animals receive a tiny portion of that just so I can maintain contact. That connection is similar to your umbilical cord, but in a cosmic and spiritual fashion, which at maturity becomes your soul and by which you are measured and judged during and at the completion of your journey.*

"That sounds like an implanted chip."

Oh yeah, good observation. You guys didn't have implantable chips a few years ago, so I didn't really make the connection. Very good. This in no way controls what you do in life and how you behave, that is entirely up to you. At any one time I am connected to about fourteen billion beings from here and the other living planets and sense your presence constantly, although it's almost impossible to sense any particular individual. The only reason I felt you is because of your persistence and constant bellyaching. You felt like a stone on the bottom of a shoe, and I had to stop and get rid of you, in a manner of speaking. It appeared to me that you may have a legitimate gripe, and after sixty-five plus years of kvetching, I felt the need to address your grievance, if indeed that was the real issue. And don't get too excited, there are many like you, but I do admire your consistent persistence.

"Thanks for making me feel special."

No problem. Shall we continue?

"Yes, of course. With all the millions of beings being born across the quadrant, aren't you going to run out of energy at some point?"

You are thinking. I'll give you that, but the answer is no. Since I'm giving you energy, you cannot destroy it and it is returned to its point of origin upon your departure from that cosmic train of yours. Think of it as water that you use daily. It is the same water that Neanderthals drank and has remained constant for over two billion years. Same with my energy. And the Energizer bunny.

"When you get your energy back, is it checked? What I'm asking is, is there a way of telling what the user was like? Can you tell the difference between the good and the bad and do you care?"

Now you've touched a very, very sensitive area of Creation maintenance, that being the Department of Souls. We didn't have one at first, but as beings that's you and the other arrogant ones started assuming you were better than you actually are, we decided to evaluate the returning soul slivers and see where they had been and what they had wrought. Upon further evaluation it was decided that those we considered worthy, kind and good people, would be given the privilege of extending their existence in cosmic energy form. Those we deemed otherwise, would be cleansed of all their evil, their sliver placed back into the energy pool and reassigned to new arrivals. Are you following what I am saying, Mr. Architect?

"You are talking about heaven and hell, aren't you?"

In a manner of speaking, yes. It is not how your holy books describe the process but there is definitely a reward and forfeiture arrangement that has been in place for many thousands of years. The way your holy books describe it is a bit melodramatic with the burning hell fire, gnashing of teeth, constant pain and suffering, which would also be very difficult to maintain. Who would want to work in a place like that? Always blistering hot, lousy pay, some horn-headed, red-faced son of a bitch constantly yelling at you, no coffee breaks, no pension plan, and a terrible health plan with no dental coverage. Our way simply deprives the evil ones of a fantastic everlasting future as they get slowly cleansed, rinsed and reassigned. They simply cease to exist while the worthy proceed on to cosmic ecstasy. Word to the wise, be good, do good and good will be returned a hundred fold.

"That is going to take a while to sink in. Let me get this straight. Heaven and hell actually exist. Am I understanding you correctly?"

Heaven, by some definition, yes. Hell, no. It isn't the way it's written in the Bible, but it is somewhat uncomplicated. Good souls get to enjoy the wonders of Creation after the physical body is gone, but the soul, that sliver of energy you all are gifted at birth, is returned home and remains there forever. The evil ones are simply purged of their wickedness to be reissued again. Call it soul recycling.

Hold it, hold it. Wait a minute. Now I know where you get the notion of me being the Father. Somewhere in the Bible it says, 'in my Father's house are many rooms.' That writer sensed the presence of heaven, just didn't fully understand the mechanics of it all. Apparently, some of your ancients were much more astute than I realized. But I'm not anyone's Father, and there is kind of a heaven, but no hell.

"Now it's coming full circle. I finally see it. It all makes perfect sense. Essentially you don't waste your time and energy, no pun intended, on the wicked, and you bless the virtuous and the righteous."

That is pretty much it. If you should decide to share our whole conversation, make sure that it is understood that where your soul winds up is all up to each individual, nobody else.

"I'm going to have a tough time convincing people that I'm not nuts when I tell them who I've been talking to, and now on top of that, you want me to promote righteousness? In this day and age?"

You called me, remember? I am just giving you the tools to help your brethren. How and what you do, again, is up to you. I know you didn't ask for all of this, but since you were admitted into our circle, I feel it necessary to impart as much knowledge in you as I can, and hopefully you can go out there and do some good.

"You sure don't make things easy, do you?"

No.

"Well, Mr. Creator, I need some help here. How do I start? Do I share the word? Do I promote righteousness?"

That would be a start, but I see I'm going to have to spend a little more time with you than I anticipated. I would start with a brief history lesson. So many people of this time don't seem to know their history. Point out how hubris led to so many wars which in turn wound up destroying civilizations and caused millions of people to suffer and die needlessly. Take the country of Japan for instance. The people there are, by and large, one of the most intelligent, industrious, and courteous people on your planet. They have produced magnificent works of art, architecture, and engineering, but unfortunately, they also possessed an aggressiveness and a sense of superiority that caused them to invade some of their neighbors and eventually make a miscalculation of epic proportions. Their senseless aggression in World War II led to countless deaths across the world and the destruction of two of their cities with over 200,000 dead and wounded in the two bombings. Having abandoned its militaristic posturing, Japan is prosperous today. Unfortunately, that prosperity is severely challenged by that very prosperity itself as more women abandon traditional roles and concentrate on their careers rather than pursuing marriage and family. This shift in the workforce has resulted in an alarming decline in their birth rate, which they will need to address.

I still can't help but wonder what they could have achieved if they didn't take that detour into self-righteousness.

Obviously, they are not the only ones. I'm sure you know about Germany and their exploits into the realm of superiority. Perhaps you could show photographs of Dresden after the bombing. It didn't have to go that way. Tell the people to study the history of the world and ask them to imagine the possibilities of cooperation rather than conflict. As I see it, you people are close to repeating history again. Previously, I mentioned that I heard some of your various tribes have enough nuclear weapons to destroy all of mankind three times over. Of course, that begs a simple and at the same time, stupid question. How can you kill someone three times, and why would you want to possess such power? Besides, the aftermath of those weapons would eventually circle the globe and land in your own backyard. There is no getting away from it.

Remember planet 14-490?

"That's the one that you said was about two hundred thousand years behind us?"

That's right, but I didn't tell you why. It isn't because evolution was slow in their neighborhood. It was in fact, very generous to them. They were, more or less, on the same evolutionary trajectory as the guys on 14-347 and 14-444 when they, just as you have, discovered the power of the atom. Without going into too many details, they too were divided into tribes or as you call them, countries, and they all went out there trying to prove who the top dog was. After many arguments, senseless posturing and numerous threats later, weaponry appeared from their satellites, and all hell broke loose. Half of them didn't know that the other half had the same capabilities and making a sad story sadder, their actions resulted in mutual suicide.

Most of the plant life was gone, certainly most the people and just about all the animals were gone. Few of their salamanders, rats, and cockroaches, which are similar to the ones you have, remained to fill the evolutionary wagons and headed underground and underwater. Couple of hundred thousand years later, just like here, they came out of the water, caves, and burrows, and again, evolution did its thing and now they are just past the tree-dwelling stage. Ironically, every now and then, one of those satellites falls out the sky and what remnants remain, these poor creatures worship as gifts from unknown gods. Perhaps in another hundred thousand years or so, they will figure out what that big light in the sky is and why and how it disappears at night and comes back in the morning. Perhaps.

You see, Mr. Architect, technology and rockets and planes and computers and the atom are not necessarily a prescription for utopian success, as some of you believe. All those achievements can be a huge benefit but also, as indicated above, a detriment of galactic proportions. So, when you ask me where to start, you could relay this story. If you think that your folks may be a bit hesitant to believe you, try showing them pictures of Hiroshima and Nagasaki, and as I mentioned earlier, Dresden, right after the destruction, and remind them that the weapons you possess today are hundreds of times more powerful and thousands of times more abundant. For your survival, you must understand that you have a common enemy, and that enemy is your own hubris and overblown sense of self-importance. Maybe someone will listen and possibly even hear. Maybe.

There was no doubt about it. I had a monumental job ahead of me. But it sure sounded like history was the best place to start.

"I have always said that people don't study history enough. And as you know, Churchill said 'Those who fail to learn from history are condemned to repeat it.' It's tragic that you weren't in a position to do something?"

I know, but as I have reiterated before, we are not everywhere at all times, and we just don't take the side of one tribe against another. Besides, at that time we were just getting settled in, learning the ropes of Creation management, and had not gotten around to visiting all the living planets. When we came up on the scene there, the war was pretty much a forgone conclusion, and we could only watch it unfold. That's why I keep harping on your weapons of mass extinction. I know what they will do unless you people wise up and figure out how to coexist. Besides, our interventions take time and are tailored so the inhabitants don't know we are interceding.

Looking at it in a simplistic way, let's assume someone does start a war which results in, let's say, five billion casualties. Another billion will die from radiation poisoning and another billion from starvation. In that scenario, who is going to stand up and declare victory? What is it that they would have won? Perhaps they get all the gold, diamonds, and money in the world, bring it to their newly decorated cave, sit on their impressive radiation deflecting golden throne and survey all their wealth, all the while chanting, we won, we won, we won. Who are the "we?" What are they going to buy with all that money when there is nothing to buy? And at some point, they will have to venture out to find food for which there will be deadly competition.

Finally, the remainder of the "Winners" will die off due to nothingness, clutching their gold bars and their shoes filled with diamonds, chanting with their last breath, we won, we won, we wo . . .

Why don't you put together a nice colorful pie chart of the above described scenario and take it on a tour around college campuses? Maybe do a

PowerPoint presentation? Kids these days really get into that computer generated stuff.

"I'll give you this. You sure know how to paint a bleak picture."

I am not the painter, the picture paints itself.

"Let me let that sink in and think about how to best convey that message. In the meantime, I have a serious personal question, which will certainly be of interest to many of my peers. Why were we designed in a manner where old age is a burden on us older folks and on the younger ones who, at times, take care of us? Why does everything hurt when you get old? Was that really intended?"

Funny you should ask. I had that same question for A5 when he was in the midst of his animal creation task, when I noticed that older animals and eventually, you guys, were moving more slowly and were just out of sorts in your old age. He told me a very interesting fable regarding that, one that I am not sure I believe, but have no reason to doubt to him.

"Yeah, I know, you didn't want to hurt his feelings."

No, not that and don't be rude. Do you have any idea how difficult it is to find a qualified replacement angel? Of course, you don't. Nobody is perfect, so we work with what and whom we have and endeavor to improve ourselves. His explanation does have much logic to it, though.

The reason, he says, is rather simple. Everyone, at some point, has to depart the train of life and in order to prepare them for it, we make it physically difficult and painful to exist so that the idea of ending the agony, becomes appealing, and eventually you all welcome life's inevitable conclusion and the accompanying certainty of pain elimination. In essence, you look forward to getting off that train. That make sense to you?

"Actually, it does. I don't like it, but it does make sense. Now that I think about it, I had a friend, Jim, who was ninety-nine years old but was sharp as a tack, not something you would expect in a man that age, who told me, about seven or eight months before he departed, that he was tired and ready to go at any time. He was in a fair amount of pain, a lot of the parts weren't working properly anymore and some, not at all. I didn't like hearing it, but I fully understood, it was his time. I just hope that I will be that ready when my time comes."

Don't worry, you will be.

"Good to know."

"I don't suppose you know when . . . ?"

Stop right there. I don't, and even if I did, do you really think I would tell you? It would ruin whatever time you had left. Constantly counting down the days and moping around without purpose. This way, you can try to contribute to your fellow arrogants some words of wisdom you have gleaned from these last few days, in your remaining time. Got it?

"Yes, sir. Okay, I know you are antsy to go, so let me get in a few more questions before you leave. May I ask how many others you picked to interact with during this trip?"

As I recall, we came here about sixty years ago and slowly made the rounds around your planet. I had hundreds of candidates on my list and so far, I've contacted around thirty. Some encounters were not as productive as this one simply because they apparently were not convinced I was real. Then again, others, like you, took it in stride, and we had a productive exchange. We should be here for another fifty or sixty years or so, to see how you progress. We make our rounds every few thousand years to see how life is advancing on each of our life planets. When we see interesting and positive progress developing, we tend to stay longer to make sure you don't get too full of yourselves. I've mentioned some of the issues I have noticed, earlier. Anyway, you, like the others have been so resolute for many years we thought you deserved a visit. I suppose you could say there was an element of luck in each selection, but by and large, all of you were interesting and persistent. You remember when you had those blocked arteries near your heart, and you asked the doctor how it was that you were alive?

"I think I understand how you would know that, but why would you care about me?"

As I recall, his exact words were, "You are lucky. It appears that you are one of those people who are able to grow what are called collateral blood vessels to go around the blockage."

Similar situation here. You were a bit lucky, as I have millions of these requests, but you were unrelenting in your appeals in that you only wanted answers and not favors. I wanted to see for myself if you were for real, and I'm certainly glad I met you.

"Whoa! Let me let that sink in. I was not expecting that."

I told you, I call it the way it is. We've had our disagreements these last few days, but you are an interesting fellow.

"Again, thank you. If I may, I would like to get a few more questions in before you leave. Okay?"

Sure.

"With all my close calls and mistakes, it seems that I have been luckier than most. You didn't have anything to do with that, did you?"

Maybe, but that's all I'm saying.

"Thank you. Now let's get back to your trip to Brazil. You said that you and the A's are capable of increasing your presence in us through which you can experience what we see and feel. By the increased presence, I'm guessing, you mean expanding that sliver of energy you provided to us at birth, right?"

Bravo, Mr. Architect. You are continuing to impress me.

"Now, for the $64,000 question. Why did you choose the masculine form on this trip? You clearly do not have a physical body or presence of any kind that would indicate one or the other."

Another direct hit by Mr. Architect. Congratulations. We can actually present ourselves in either form if the situation called for it. Since we are going to be around for a number of years during this trip, we will take many forms, including of some animals. We have done that on other planets, and it is magical to behold the feeling of being alive. Just imagine being a tiger chasing a gazelle and understanding that you are the tiger.

"Yeah, I get it. But why go all the way to Brazil? Never mind, I know why. I've seen a number of Brazilian women. I've met a couple of them."

I'm glad you figured it out. What is there to explain? Even one as geezerly as you can appreciate that kind of beauty.

"Ooh! Another one below the belt. I'll be the bigger man and let that one go for now. Since you are looking to get rid of me, let me get back to something you said earlier. You told me that when you were assigned the task of Creation, you had to figure out the how, where, and when, but the concept of why presented itself much, much later."

That is correct, much later.

"Right. So, what is the answer? Why was all this created?"

I knew that one would come sooner or later, but I'm afraid I will have to leave you disappointed.

To get that answer, you will have to ask God.

"What? Ask God? Then who the hell are you? I thought you were God."

Why would you think that? I told you who I was from the start. Didn't I?

"You said you were the Creator, and you knew damn well that we were all taught God and the Creator were one and the same. Why would you not tell me that at the beginning? Now you are going to tell me that He is some other cluster of energy, right?"

Well, yes, but I would not refer to Him as "some other cluster." He is The Cluster. Get that through your thick Serbian skull. He doesn't play. If you piss him off, He will smite and smite hard. You think I'm overbearing and domineering, you should hear Him. When we screwed up the First Burst, He almost fired me, but lucky for me, the other Creators were all too busy working their own Creations that He didn't have any choice but to keep me. But to be fair, when you do well, He is very generous. And by the way, He really is not a he, she, or it. I use that reference so you would understand what I'm talking about, but "He" is the ultimate energy cluster and the absolute, dare I say, "Master Architect" of all.

"Wow, Master Architect, that has a nice ring to it. But wait. What do you mean, other Creators? How many of you clusters are out there?"

Six more and me. All told, seven. And six more Universes for another total of seven. Are you sure you want to hear more?

"Why didn't you tell me all this in the beginning? Seven Universes? What's with this seven obsession?"

That again would be a question for the Master. Just so you understand, He doesn't talk to whoever prays, that's what we are for, and let me tell you, we are overwhelmed with prayers and requests.

"Oh, that's a riot. You are his buffer, his consigliere, his confidant. I love it."

His buffer, yes, not really his confidant, but we do communicate from time to time.

"Okay, be straight with me, I know he told you why He started all this and now that seven Universes are in play, I'm certain he divulged the why. Tell me."

Here it is, but people are not going to believe you. He told me that He is looking for a pure and honest soul. A few have come close, but none has made it to the top.

So long Architect, be well.

Made in the USA
Monee, IL
07 July 2021